Keeping up
with Kaneda

Keeping up with Kaneda

GAURAV KUMAR

Srishti
PUBLISHERS & DISTRIBUTORS

Srishti Publishers & Distributors
Registered Office: N-16, C.R. Park
New Delhi – 110 019
Corporate Office: 212A, Peacock Lane
Shahpur Jat, New Delhi – 110 049
editorial@srishtipublishers.com

First published by
Srishti Publishers & Distributors in 2018

To,
Papaji and Dadima,
Thank you for being a part of my life.
I am extremely fortunate to have been your grandchild.

Hari Om!

Prologue…
Hmm, how do I begin?

Well, I can start by telling you what this book is about.

For one, it is a light-hearted and fun read.

It is an experiential journey into the life of a guy (me!) who has recently moved to a 'foreign' country. It is the search for a good temporary job, the oddities, the people, the fun and the various quirks of Canada as a country from an Indian's perspective.

And a few unique experiences as well!

So, you can sit back with a nice, tall glass of your favourite beverage and read on. Oh! one more thing.

I dedicate this book to my wife Hansika whose constant support and encouraging feedback kept me going. Also, to my cousin Vaibhav and chaddi buddies Koushik, Mohta, Bagla, Jha, Anuj, Randhir, Pandey, Shubham, Mohit for their endless *bakchodi*, fun and frolic. To, Tsultem, Neha and Viral for their superb reactions to my initial drafts.

And finally, to my parents and lil' sis for being who they are.

Ancestral Traits

So, I am super excited! My plane is finally landing in Toronto; the city which I thought would turn my life around, thanks to its relaxed visa norms and exciting multicultural experiences.

I literally have goose bumps as the airhostess says, "Welcome to Toronto. It is minus ten degrees outside and very windy. Please be sure to have your winter jackets on when you leave the plane."

Then I realize that I probably got goose bumps because the door of the plane had been opened for the passengers to exit and the beautiful weather was filtering inside.

Aah! Well, welcome to '*Kaneda*' as the Punjabis say!

My cousin Richa and her husband Krupal have come to pick me up at the airport. I am meeting them after a period of almost ten years. Needless to say, she literally jumps on me when I enter the passenger arrival area which thankfully is indoors, unlike Mumbai airport.

Richa: "*Bhaiiiii*!!! Welcome to Toronto! How was your flight?! Wait, open your suitcase first and take out your warm clothes, winter cap and scarf."

Me: "Richaaa! Kya haal hai? It's been so long. The flight was good, stopover was at Amsterdam, which I only got to see through the large frosted airport windows; thanks to an Indian passport which requires one to have a visa wherever in the world one might need to travel (except Nepal I think, but I'm not too sure). Tanked up on a lot of booze on the flight!"

Richa goes ahead and opens my suitcase, taking out my winter clothes and orders me to wear them, complete with the woolen scarf and skull cap which makes me look like one of those guys on their way to climb Mount Everest.

Krupal: "Great to see you dude, chal I'll give you a little heads up on how this city works."

Well, you see, my brother-in-law is a guy who comes straight to the point in any situation.

Me (in my sleep deprived yet excited state): "Sure, I'm all ears. I'm like a sponge who will adapt to this city better than the people who have lived here all their lives."

Krupal goes on to explain to me how the Toronto public transport system and road system work while we are on our way to their house. I'm just looking out of the window, having a Shah Rukh Khan moment where he says that one day he will own this city. Yes, a little cheesy, but that's how excited I was!

So, we reach their apartment building. It's almost 11 p.m. and all I can see is thick white snow all around me. It was the last week of December. I have never seen real snow before, not even in India. I have seen like fake snow at Dream World in Bangkok where they cool a gigantic room below zero, but still it was nothing like I expected.

As soon as we step out of the taxi, I feel a sensation on my face which I have never experienced before. It felt like cold needles pricking me on my cheeks, making my nose red and watery. (I felt somehow sympathetic to Rudolf – the red-nosed reindeer, who comes from the North Pole). It is super windy, and not the monsoon wind like back in Mumbai but the kind that can literally freeze you in your place if you don't move your ass. Hauling our bags, we run inside the building. Their rented apartment is on the tenth floor which also has the landlord living in the adjoining room. As soon as we enter the house, we are greeted by a guy watching TV, who suddenly turns and looks in my direction.

Guy: "Hi, I'm Sameer. Welcome to Toronto! Are you from Gujarat?"

Me: "Huh? Umm... Hi, I'm Gaurav. No I'm from Maharashtra, Bombay actually."

Sameer: "Mumbai! *Arre waah saaro chhe*. Did Krupal explain to you how the metro and the road system work here? It's nothing like Mumbai. It is very organized, clean and safe. Sit down, I'll tell you all about it!"

Well, this is the first little observation I have made in Toronto. I am not stereotyping but my brother-in-law and Sameer both happen to be Gujarati. *Gujjus* living here, it seems, like to take charge of anyone who arrives completely new in the country by giving them little tips, dos, don'ts, where to buy the cheapest groceries, where to get great Indian food, etc. To me, it seems like an ancestral trait which has been passed on by generations of NRIs who were constantly welcoming people from India and helping them settle 'the right way' in a foreign land.

Me: "Sure Sameer, in a bit. I'll just call my parents and tell them I've reached here safe and sound."

Suddenly the doorbell rings and a couple enters. The guy introduces himself as Abhijeet and the girl as Paulomi. Abhijeet looks very happy to see everyone, rather a little too happy. Paulomi starts looking for something in the kitchen. She comes out with a bottle of wine. I then realize that this is going to be a long, long night. Both are nearly drunk and start filling up the glasses. Sameer keeps saying that he can drink a dime a dozen, but the drink never gets to him.

After a glass of wine, he's as drunk as both of them. Sameer and Abhijeet start with their stories of how they had arrived in the big city and how they got their PR. Well, for those of you who don't know, PR stands for Permanent Residency in Canada and it's the pot of gold at the end of the rainbow – the coveted prize which sets apart Indians from... umm well other Indians. For me, it's all very fascinating, but the nineteen-hour flight kinda makes you a little tired. By this time, all the guys have started singing a particular popular Hindi song sung by a Pakistani singer hitting all the high notes with such enthusiasm that even I join in for some odd reason. Richa understands that I need to sleep and slyly points towards the bedroom while distracting them so that I can slip away. I love my cousin. Beautiful sleep, here I come!

Well, the reason I have come to Toronto is to do a super-condensed programme in Strategic Management in a very popular community college. The duration of the whole programme is eight months, making it very intense, a bit like MBA on steroids. Community college because fees are one-tenth of a private college and almost on par with the fees of a similar programme in India. And because I didn't want any hassle of a gigantic student loan dangling like a sword over my neck and to put unnecessary pressure on me or my parents.

I had pre-decided that I would completely support myself financially without asking for any monetary help from my parents by doing odd/temp jobs when I was not studying or attending college.

Well, I finally wake up around 9 a.m. next morning and everyone is shocked because not only do I not experience jet lag, but also I wake up quite cheery and well rested. Sameer is still sleeping and Richa is almost ready to leave for work. She gives me a big hug and says that she'll call me in the evening. Krupal suggests I finish breakfast quickly so that he can drop me to my shared accommodation near my college. Breakfast is *dhoklas* with *chutney* and *chai* which are a bit of a surprise because ignorant me was thinking that my first breakfast in Toronto will be a typical Canadian one – complete with pancakes with maple syrup, sausages, bagels with cream cheese and Tim Hortons' coffee. Well for those who don't know – Tim Hortons is to Canada what Cafe Coffee Day is to India. It's literally in every corner of every street and surprisingly very affordable, unlike Starbucks.

Anyway, so I gobble up my 'Canadian' breakfast and head for the shower. Krupal makes himself busy reading the newspaper and asking me to hurry up because he has an interview lined up at 2 p.m. that afternoon. I get dressed for my Mount Everest expedition again, seeing the amount of snow outside.

The shared accommodation where I'll be moving into is a house about a kilometre away from my college and is one of three owned by a Gujju. The first three houses are for students and the last house is the landlord's. We walk into his office which is in the basement of his house. We are overwhelmed by the sight of about three hundred frames dangling from the walls on each side. Closer inspection reveals that they are all certificates and degrees of this highly learned man.

Landlord: "Myself Bhavesh Shah. Welcome to Torentu. Your rent is six hunred dollar for single room, given to me by you in advance. Only then I'll open the room. All lunches and dinners foods included and timing is strictkkly punctuual, if you want fooding in time. I also lawyer many students for PR so you can come to me anytime if you want to have PR."

Krupal nudges me to ask if I have understood everything that he said and I wink to say it's all good. I've had my fair share of 'learned' English speaking folks back at home. My journey to the other side has begun!

After paying the rent 'in advance', I carry my bags to my room, the tiniest room I've seen in my life. It is inside a small house which is divided into about four rooms on the ground floor and four rooms in the basement. Only my room is single sharing, the rest are double sharing and triple sharing, all of which are occupied. That's about sixteen people in one house. As Russell Peters said, the guy was 'minting money!'

P.S.: I came to know later that all of Mr Bhavesh Shah's houses were raided by the Toronto Fire Department and sealed because it was a huge safety hazard as well as illegal to allow so many people to live under one roof.

Is you DJ?

$\mathcal{I}$ move out of Mr Bhavesh Shah's house after a month with a few friends from college. We get a two bedroom flat near college for almost less than half what we were paying to Mr Bhavesh.

So I, Vishal, Mathew and Shirish (my roomies) are sitting in the living room of our new house having our daily constructive debate. Well, you see the Tamilians I live with loved to argue, give their opinion and discuss just about everything under the sun. We Punjabis usually only do that after we've had a peg or two!

Mathew and Shirish are usually on the opposite sides of the argument and end up having a heated debate.

Vishal cracks up at the way the discussion is progressing while I am trying to look for a temp job as usual on Kijiji and Craigslist. College is on in full swing and I am thinking of getting a part-time job to support my living expenses in Toronto. For those who don't know both Kijiji and Craigslist, those are free classified websites similar to OLX or Quikr in India.

Suddenly, my phone rings and a heavily accented guy introduces himself as Carlos. Carlos (in terrible English): "Hey is you DJ? Your friend tell me about you."

Me: "Err...yes me is... I mean, yeah, I DJ." (One of my talents since my engineering days. I used to DJ at a pub called Thousand Oaks in Pune.)

Carlos: "That's good! Come to my club downtown, Church and Wellesley. Three hours you play I pay you. My regular cancel today. Will you come my place?"

Okay. Now I am excited. I would be DJing in a club in downtown Toronto! What!? Damn I couldn't believe my luck!

Me: "Sure, I'm in. What is your club called?"

Carlos: "Chikoroo. Come 7 p.m. today evening. I text myself to you."

Me (thinking, how the fuck can people speak such bad English and survive in this English speaking country): "Ok, thanks."

I turn to Vishal and say, "Are you in for a MAD night?"

Vishal: "Who was that?"

Me: "Some guy called Carlos. He told me to come down to his club called Chikoroo and deejay there. Google it, let's see how the place is."

Vishal pulls out his laptop and we google the place. It's not a club but a small restaurant which turns into a pub in the evening with the chairs and tables put outside.

Ah well, I think, should be an interesting experience.

We reach the place at half past six and are greeted by Carlos who looks every bit like a clichéd Columbian drug dealer, like the ones we see in Hollywood movies. And to top that, Carlos is his name! He has a flowery shirt with a massive collar which was partly unbuttoned, allowing his chest hair to wave at the person in front of him. And he is wearing a thick gold chain around his neck.

Yup, *you do not mess* with Carlos.

Carlos: "Guravey! Welcome to Chikoroo. Like place?"

Me: "Hi Carlos! It's Gaurav actually. Yes, I'm looking forward to playing here. This is my first official proper gig in Toronto other than a few house parties. This is my friend Vishal, he will be assisting me."

I nudge Vishal to introduce himself, but he seems mesmerized by Carlos's chest hair, waving back at him.

Carlos (gives Vishal a small pat on his cheek and points to the corner): "Nice nice. Me too. You can DJ from there."

We proceed to the corner to set up. I, for some odd reason, have a funny feeling about the place. I just cannot put my finger on it.

Vishal: "Did you see the sign board kept on the floor outside? It says DJ Sugar Daddy is playing tonight! Hahahahaha, dude you are tainted for life now! We have a new nickname for you now. Wait, lemme call Mathew and Shirish."

Me: "Asshole! What the fuck! I swear there won't be any free drinks for you tonight if you tell them or anyone for that matter."

Vishal: "Hahahaha, ok! Ok relax. Put some sugar on it."

Me: "You say that one more time and I'll kick you in the nuts. Then, you can put all the sugar you want on them!"

The place is mostly empty except for two girls chatting away in one corner and about five guys doing a few shots at the bar. They seem very happy and are hugging each other.

I start with my set, while Vishal is nursing his drink and contemplating on going over to talk to the girls. A few people start to trickle inside around 8 p.m. The place is moderately packed now.

Suddenly, two male waiters appear holding trays filled with jello shots in one hand and sparklers in the other and climb on top of a table.

Any other time, I would not be surprised by this; the only difference now is that the waiters are wearing thongs.

Yes, you read that right. Male waiters wearing *only* thongs!

Suddenly I realize what the fuck was odd about the place. I look around – all guys. This is a gay club. It is at this moment I see Vishal as flabbergasted at the turn of events as I am.

His look says it all. Pure shock.

A girl in a mini skirt walks up to my booth, who upon closer inspection turns out to be a transvestite. She/He seems to be talking to me. I snap out of my daze.

Girl/Guy: "Hi cutie, can you play some of Lady Gaga's tracks?"

Me:....

Girl/Guy: "Darling, can you hear me?! I said can you play some of Lady Gaga's tracks?"

Me: "Oh... huh... Ok."

Girl/Guy grins and walks off to her/his group of friends. I notice that Vishal is staring at me. His mind is still trying to process the sudden change of events. He probably thought that he would *patao* a cute chick while pretending to be my side-kick and sweet talk his way to paradise. Aspirations kick in the nuts by reality. I continue my set, including a few Lady Gaga tracks which receive a huge round of whistles and cheering. Alcohol is definitely helping take the edge off as I acclimatize. People around me are talking, laughing, enjoying, kissing, etc. I too engage in a conversation with an Irish guy who says that he comes here often on the weekends with his pals as he likes the way the owner treats everyone. Everyone is welcome at Chikoroo – whatever your inclination is! From the corner of my eye, I see Vishal walking towards me with two guys. He is grinning.

Vishal: "Dude! I just got you your next gig. These guys are getting married next week and I convinced them that you should deejay at their wedding. Am I awesome or what?"

Me: "Asshole! One shocker at a time, huh. But good work, your managing skills are improving."

Vishal: "So my commission is set, boss! Let's play more Lady Gaga!"

P.S.: I do finally end up deejaying at the wedding party which Vishal had fixed. Pretty epic party, I must say.

We buy gold?
We sell diamonds??

$\mathcal{S}$o, in my constant pursuit of finding a part time job that pays well, this one goes back to the time when I had just arrived in Toronto.

I was browsing through Craigslist looking for a part time job when I saw this ad for a jewellery store offering to pay twenty bucks an hour for advertising their products. The ad said the person must be 'healthy' and must be willing to work hard.

Hey, I think, I am both! I called them and set an appointment to meet.

They are located in the industrial district belt of Toronto, and are not like a regular jewellery store. They looked more like a pawn shop. Well, FYI a pawn shop is a place where you can sell almost anything for cold, hard cash.

On reaching there, the store manager said that I fit the bill as I was tall and would attract attention. I am having all sorts of crazy ideas in my head as to what the job would be. The manager then tells me to wait and goes inside and brings what looks like a big placard with their store name printed on it. On the front of the card it says that 'WE BUY GOLD! DROP

BY OUR STORE AT ****' and on the back it said 'AND WE SELL DIAMONDS TOO! COME AND SAY HI AT OUR STORE AT ****'

Me: "Do I have to hold this card over my head or something?"

Manager: "No, of course not! You have to wear it. I will come and randomly check up on you to see if you are doing it well or not."

Me: "Err… I have to wear it?"

Manager: "Exactly."

He goes on to show me it is actually called a sandwich board which is basically two placards fitted together on top and a cavity on one side through which a head could pass through so it looks like I am wearing a cheap sort of armour on my body. He instructs me to put it on.

Manager: "There you go! Now you just have to walk around on the street for about half a kilometre and smile. I will see you back after ten hours."

Me: "Ten hours?! I am just supposed to walk around wearing this for ten hours?"

Manager: "Exactly."

So off I go. I thought to myself that this should be a piece of cake. All I have to do is walk around for ten hours and get paid. Easiest money ever! Well, they say there is no such thing as a free lunch and I was going to get hit by the reality bus.

I manage to get through the first two hours just smiling and walking around. Plenty of folks would walk by and smile back, or crack jokes like, 'Hey, rich guy! Do you give us poor folks a discount?' or 'What's the price of gold today?!' or even the outrageous 'My wife would love to meet you!'

I am thoroughly enjoying myself. And then at the end of the third hour, boredom hit me. The hours drags on and I am bored out of my wits. I decide that something needs to be done or else I would not be able to do this job for three straight days. I call up two friends of mine from college and tell them that I am working at this place and they needed two more people for the job. The only downside I told them is that it would pay them a lump sum of forty bucks each for a job entailing them to stand for about ten hours.

Since they have nothing better to do and would be earning a few bucks too, they are delighted and say that they were in!

So, Divya and Shyam arrive to see me walking around wearing a sandwich board and start cracking up. And then it suddenly hit them. They would have to do the same thing.

Me: "*Aao saalon*! Let's do some sandwich boarding!"

Divya: "Gaurav!? I can't do this. This is so embarrassing. How are you doing it?"

Me: "Hey, it's not so bad once you wear it. Here you go!"

She looks all red in the face and I and Shyam are laughing our asses off!

Me: "Shyam, you are next buddy."

Suddenly, for Shyam, things are not so funny anymore. I am thoroughly enjoying myself. Not only is this more fun but also when three people are doing the same thing, time goes by more swiftly. Before we know it, 'our' ten hours were over. We chat with people on the street, play UNO awhile and also go for a few beers. Getting paid for doing all this sounds like a perfect temp job!

So, I am back into the 'jewellery shop'. I enter and see the manager speaking in hushed tones to a lady who looks like his boss.

Manager: "You are fired."

Me: "I am fired?"

Manager: "Exactly."

As you can see, the manager is a man of few words and 'exactly' was his favourite.

Boss Woman: "You looked like you were having fun out there. Who were those two other people?"

Me: "Shit. I didn't think you guys would actually keep an eye on me the whole time. They are friends of mine. I could manage the first three hours but I was bored like I have never been before. So, I called a few friends of mine and offered to split my pay with them."

Boss Woman: "And I'm guessing you didn't tell them the actual amount I was gonna pay you."

I'm thinking how the hell does she know that!

Boss Woman: "Anyway, here's your money. Someday you will make a good manager, I feel. For now, you're fired."

P.S.: Well, you know what they say, "If you aren't fired with enthusiasm, you will be fired with enthusiasm." (Quote: Vince Lombardi.)

Yo dude, park my Beemer, will ya?

My weekdays are usually spent in my college, submitting assignments, giving reports and presentations. Late afternoon and evening times are usually free. Hence, I would try to find temporary jobs that allow me to work within that time frame.

My cousin Richa calls me up one day and tells me she might have a job for me. Richa works at an HR agency and would often call me to let me know if there are any openings available that would suit me.

I have to reach an elite country club called Granite which is located on Bayview Avenue in Toronto.

She tells me to meet the valet supervisor there at 7 p.m. who will explain to me more about the job.

I reach Granite around half past six and enter the club through the staff entrance. I am directed to go to the first level of the underground parking area where I am supposed to meet Mr Blaise. As I am walking towards the parking area, I cannot help but notice the sheer amount of cars waiting to enter.

It turns out that the club is hosting a Diwali 'gala', which is an exclusive invitee only event attended by who's who of Toronto.

Mr Blaise is a tall, lanky skeleton of a man who in my opinion has spent too much time underground, literally.

Blaise instructs me that all I have to do is to guide the drivers of the cars waiting to the empty parking slots starting from the lowest level, working my way up. I am also introduced to another person called Vishnu, a Sri Lankan chap, who will also be doing the same job as me.

Me and Vishnu make our way down to the lower levels and wait for the cars to come.

Vishnu: "My man, you have a very unique name. What does it mean?"

Me: "Gaurav means pride, although half the *firangs* in Toronto are unable to pronounce it. I think I understand now, why many South Asians change their name here to make it more accent-friendly."

Vishnu: "I know what you mean man, although my name is easier on the tongue. This Jamaican girl I was with last night, kept screaming my name as I was giving her head. I felt like god, all powerful and invincible!

Me: "Whoa dude! Slow down, what? I thought we were talking about names!"

Vishnu: "Yea man, she was screaming it like she was on a rodeo or something. Stamina like a horse, that one!"

Vishnu proceeds to ride an imaginary horse imitating the girl. I am laughing so hard that I do not hear a car honking behind me waiting to be guided to a parking spot.

I compose myself and start with the job. Vishnu on the other hand is still riding the horse, oblivious to the people staring at him.

Me: "*Oye*, Vishnu! What the fuck are you doing? Get to work man, there are people waiting here."

Vishnu: "Oh, my bad, bro!" (Proceeds towards a waiting car). "Hi girl, how are you this lovely evening? This is a nice car you have here, shiny as a baby's bottom."

Girl in the car: "Hi, if you don't mind, can you please park my car? I am already running late!"

Vishnu: "Sure thing, my lady. You are the queen and I am your stable boy. I shall do as you please and I shall be gentle!"

This guy is out of control. First, the Jamaicans and now the stupid sexual innuendos. This is going to be an interesting night.

Girl in the car: "Hey asshole, fuck off. I see a space right there!"

She uses a few more colourful words for Vishnu before proceeding towards the empty slot. Her night has already had an interesting start to it, it seems.

Me: "Vishnu, what's with the pervy comments? You high or something?"

Vishnu: "I'm baked as an apple pie bro. Real nice Jamaican weed. Fuck, I am hungry too. Let's go have some munchies after we deal with these uptight asses here."

Me: "Yea, me too, a little bit. Let's go after we finish."

The cars just keep pouring in and we keep moving from level to level until we reach the top to see a very worried Mr Blaise.

Blaise (speaking to us): "Can either of you guys drive?"

Me: "Sure, I can."

Vishnu: "No way, I can't drive to save my life. I once drove an old Toyota…"

Blaise (cutting him off): "That's great Garoo. From now on, since the parking is full, you tell the folks to leave their keys inside the vehicle and make them double park. When someone leaves, we park their vehicle in that slot. Understood?"

Me: "Yes, sir."

I could not control my excitement! In front of me, I could see a long line of Audis, Mercs, Beemers and Range Rovers. This night is truly turning out to be pretty legendary.

Right, so let the game begin! It is a dream come true for me to be driving so many cars in one night, even though for a short distance.

It takes us roughly about two hours to ensure that we had double parked, even triple parked the cars. We left the keys in the ignition in case we needed to move them again. Needless to say, after all that 'hard work', I am famished. Vishnu, surprisingly, wrapped up his work too without any major incident.

We decide to head to the staff kitchen to grab a bite. It is a minimal spread but delicious nonetheless. Roast chicken, peas and mashed sweet potato. We hog and hog till we could almost eat no more.

After eating we must have just sat there in the glory of our amazing meal for about half an hour when Vishnu 'ji' has a eureka idea.

He suggested we crash the party upstairs and hit the dessert buffet. Apparently, his 'munchies' are kicking in again. I'm sold. After a delicious meal, no one can say no to dessert. Let alone a dessert buffet!

We sneak our way past the security using the internal staff staircase, through the main hall area and land up in the main dining area of the event. Luckily, most of the guests are still inside the main hall area drinking and are being 'educated' about Diwali and Indian rituals and customs.

The staff in the massive dining area is sparse too as they are not expecting people to come in for another hour at least. We dash towards the dessert section and boy o' boy is it massive. Every dessert, sweet dish, treat you can think of, is here. From lip-smacking tiramisu to exquisite pavlova to godly rasgullas. Nutella pancakes, *rabri* with *jalebi*, macarons and even a triple layer chocolate cake, real vanilla ice cream, phew!

If this was my last day on earth, I would happily spend it within the confines of this very room.

Overloading our plates (We decide that the dessert plates provided are too small, so obviously, we get the main course dinner plates), we start making our way back to the staff staircase to enjoy our loot in case someone catches us in the dining area. There is only one issue. We have to pass through the main hall, with exceptionally overloaded plates in our hands.

We rack our brains, well mostly I, because Vishnu is too stoned to think, and decide that we will walk through the main hall holding the plates up like 'waiters carrying trays'.

And most importantly, keeping our cool and not rushing, to avoid attracting unwanted attention.

I tell Vishnu to walk behind me and follow my lead as we step into the fire, with our plates held high.

Snaking our way through the guests, I breathe a sigh of relief as almost everyone is busy looking at a dance performance organized by the club to pay any attention to us.

I even manage to stop for a small bite of the macaron to keep my energy going towards our goal. With the door to the staff staircase in sight, I am delirious.

When suddenly, I see Vishnu dash right past me at full speed holding his plate to his chest like his life depends on it.

Well, let's rewind back a few minutes to find out what has caused this picturesque scenario to occur.

Turns out that Vishnu, in his stony daze, ends up sitting on one of the chairs reserved for some VVIP guests.

He sits there for a very important reason – to enjoy the dance performance, with a large plate full of desserts in his hand.

So engrossed is he in the performance that he is just about to think of himself as a dignitary and feast on dessert plate that he is holding so tenderly when there is a tap on his shoulder.

Security guy: "Excuse me sir, but may I see your invite?"

Vishnu: …

Security guy: "Sir, I'm afraid, I'm gonna have to escort you outside."

Vishnu: …

Vishnu gets up only to run in my direction where I am happily oblivious to the turn of events.

Too shocked to react, I turn around to see that three guards are running towards us with angry faces. Shit! I abandon my dessert plate pocketing a few macrons and a slice of the chocolate cake and start running like mad. Vishnu has decided that he will run this marathon with his dessert plate and its contents all over his shirt.

The plate must not lose its sanctity.

The plate must survive!

We manage to run down the staff staircase and out through the back door of the venue. Hiding behind the garbage bins, we see the guards run past us screaming at the top of their voices. We sit still for another half an hour and jump a wall to a small alley and onto a random bus to the nearest metro station. An hour later, I reach home.

On our way back, Vishnu passes out in the train, his shirt now multi-coloured and edible.

The next day, I'm fired.

I don't know about Vishnu, but I have a strong feeling that they mustn't be too fond of him either.

P.S.: My favourite from the night was the BMW M3 which roared like a demon waiting to be unleashed.

Fast Company

$\mathcal{H}$i there,

If you have call centre experience and can start work this Friday, 17th December, ****, from 9:00 a.m. to 5:00 p.m., here is what you need to do:

1) Email an updated copy of your resume to ***********@*****.net

2) Come to our office to register on Thursday 16th December, 2010 between 10 a.m. – 4 p.m. at 90 Sheppard Avenue East Suite No. ***, North York, ON, M2N 3A1. Ask for Nikos (Name changed for obvious reasons)

Please register by tomorrow, 16th Thursday, December,, **** between 10:00 a.m. – 4:00 p.m.

We need twenty Call Centre Representatives who are committed to work in North York near Don Mills & ******. You will be paid $12.25/hour. Freshers may apply.

Remember, no jeans and running shoes, and you must dress professionally.

Also bring a piece of photo ID and your SIN card.

Thanks,

Nikos Tzakas

Recruitment Consultant

***** Professional Services

I wake up one extremely cold winter morning to this. Toronto is almost always cold except during their short spring and summers.

Summers are a time in Toronto for people to really appreciate god's amazing creation – the sun.

The city really undergoes a drastic transformation during summers. People stop being hermits and literally spend their entire day outdoors, whether sunbathing or barbeque in their backyard, playing in the park, simply having nice cold beer on their porch, aah the good life!

Sorry for having gone off topic there, but summers in Toronto or Canada as a whole are really something one should experience once in their lifetime. It is simply beautiful to watch the entire country come out of its prolonged winter spell and really enjoy the natural beauty that this amazing country has to offer. Winters in Toronto are super long, for literally about seven months including autumn. So, one has no option but to get used to a constant minus two to minus eight degrees on good days.

Anyway, back to my email. So, this recruitment agency contacts me with a temp job which sounds like a call centre position. I had met Nikos at some job fair and passed him my email id in case he has any positions available.

So, I revert with my resume and I am informed an hour later that the company for which I will be working is called Rocket Sales Search (name changed for obvious reasons).

I have to show up on 21st December at their office at 9 a.m. The lady on the phone strictly emphasizes on 'no jeans and running shoes'. Ok, then.

I am up quite early on *the day*. I step outside my room to see my roomie Rod who's an Australian guy, cooking breakfast. The place where I'm living now is a quaint little beautiful house. It is owned by a Canadian, with a Romanian, Australian and an Indian living in it. Rod is an excellent cook, a travel enthusiast and an overall super fun guy. Bogdan, the Romanian, is an anti-consumerist and a hater of 'the man'.

'The man' is any corporation whose sole aim is to create mass consumerism, create unnecessary wants and make people think that they have to have a particular thing to be happy.

A lot of times, however, it would turn out to be a kill joy. For example, one day, Bogdan is telling me another story of how 'the man' was ruining our lives whilst I am eating eggs for breakfast. Suddenly, he tells me that eggs are the period of the chicken and how eggs now are mass produced and chickens are genetically modified to have more 'periods' in order to produce more eggs.

Well, that sure makes my appetite go for a toss.

Developed countries have suddenly opened up to this new market of organic, pesticide-free and non-genetically modified foods since a past couple of years. I mean for us living in developing countries, ignorance is bliss and if we were to really get into how our food is sourced, people would literally stop eating. We are so used to living in ignorance, that we do not mind even eating at a roadside joint whose food is tasty even though that joint is just above a gutter and we can see all the waste, garbage flowing into that gutter in front of us.

I mean, how many times we have experienced that!

One evolutionary trait which Indians have is that have we simply mastered the art of ignorance.

Rod is the complete opposite of Bogdan. He is a super happy-go-lucky-guy, who loves to live in the moment and travel and experience new things. He finds joy in simple things, which we usually ignore.

He is thirty-four years old and has been traveling since the age of eighteen. He has literally been around the world!

Rod's agenda is, during the time, to bring in Christmas with a Canadian family. He is on the lookout for a family who would allow him to be a part of their celebrations and let him celebrate and experience Christmas, the Canadian way. Later that week, he met a kind old lady who invited him to celebrate Christmas with her entire family and it was one of the best experiences of his life!

Anyway, so back to my story.

Wearing formal attire, I reach the mentioned address, a bus and a train ride later. It is located in a business park. The office is located on the twelfth floor. I enter the office to see a smiling receptionist, sipping her coffee.

Receptionist: "Good morning!"

Me: "Hi, good morning. My name is Gaurav, today is my first day here."

Receptionist: "Hi 'Gurav', I'm Jessica. Please go to Conference Room B. The orientation for the freshers will begin shortly."

Me(thinking why the heck can't anyone pronounce my name correctly): "Thanks, Jessica."

I head to the conference room. On entering, I see a few people have already occupied their seats and the chairs in the room are divided into management in the first couple of rows, accounting in the centre and executives in the last three rows. I take a seat in the executives' row. Slowly, people start pouring in and the room is now completely packed. A guy, who introduces himself as the director of the company, starts the keynote speech emphasizing on the principles of the company and how they will change the world.

He goes on for about twenty minutes after which we, executives, are asked to report to Mr Walsh to begin our orientation.

Mr Walsh is a gregarious man, with a shiny bald head and laughs like Santa Claus. He asks each one of us our names and our strengths and why would we like to join this company. On my turn, I elaborate on my goals and my strengths sprinkled with a little bit of 'bakchodi'. Walsh appears mighty pleased with everyone. I and another girl Farah, are selected to be on the analytics team and report to Mrs Michelle. The rest of the group is segregated to be on the telesales, customer feedback and reporting team. We are told to take a break of fifteen minutes and then meet our respective supervising managers.

I am filling my coffee from the coffee machine when Farah comes up to me.

Farah: "Hi Gaurav, how's your day going so far?"

Me: "Hi, it's going ok, that Walsh guy was an interesting chap. Reminded me of Santa Claus."

Farah: "Haha, I know right! He reminded me of my sweet uncle Hamid back home. I am new to Canada. I came here last month only, from Abu Dhabi."

Me: "Oh that's great. I guess you must be still acclimating to the weather – from a super hot country to a super cold one!"

Farah: "It's been a shock for me, Gaurav. I love my country but my father had to move here due to work. We might be shifting to Saskatchewan soon, which is even colder, I've heard, so I'm dreading moving there."

Me: "Saskatchewan! Damn!! That is one of the coldest states in Canada. I am from India, been here for over eight months now. I am studying here as well as working part time. Although, I don't understand what exactly we have to do here."

Farah: "I had a quick word with Michelle, and she told me that since it is our first day, our duties will be fairly limited. She's flown in from Ottawa today morning only."

Me: "That sounds great; today will be a relaxed day then."

Mrs Michelle is in the middle of an argument over the phone when we enter the room. She suddenly stops arguing when she sees us and curtly gestures towards the door to tell us to go outside and wait for her to come.

A good fifteen minutes later, she comes outside her office and simply brushes past us to go into Walsh's office. We try to overhear the conversation, but all we can hear are muffled sounds of Michelle screaming her ass off. Walsh appears to be fairly composed and is trying to calm the situation.

We have no option but to sit at our desks and wait till we know what to do next. I feel a hand touching my shoulder and I turn around to see Mrs Michelle standing behind us.

Mrs Michelle: "Something urgent had come up and hence, I was a little pre-occupied. Anyway, welcome to Rocket Sales Search. I'm sure you must be familiar with Google Earth software?"

Me (Wow, no greetings/salutations?): "Yes, I have used it quite a bit during my engineering days for a few civil engineering assignments."

Farah: "I have heard about it, haven't used it yet."

Mrs Michelle (frowning slightly): "No problem Farah, I'll have Gurave run you through it."

She did not even have the courtesy of asking me. Not that I would have refused or anything, but I thought she was one of the rudest people I've met.

For those who don't know, Google Earth is a brilliant piece of software that allows one to view the three dimensional view of locations, buildings, landscapes to a fairly accurate degree. It was discontinued for a little while before being relaunched, although it is not very popular today as Google Maps has evolved to include many features which earlier were only limited to Google Earth.

Mrs Michelle tells us that one of their clients is a roofing company and they want to target potential customers which have a higher percentage of adopting their product. So, our job was to find out in GTA (Greater Toronto Area), houses which had large rooftops at least fifteen feet in length. She goes on to explain the beauty of Google Earth. It allows us to zoom in over a house and using the 'scale' feature, we can see the approximate dimensions of the house from every direction. And it is scarily accurate.

I have used it to locate my area in Mumbai, my building shape appears to be accurate from top view but it is flat as the three dimensional feature is only available in developed countries.

So, we are given a target of a hundred buildings and houses which we have to locate within GTA and then save the addresses on an excel sheet. Rocket Sales Search will then get the contact details of those houses and will pass the leads to the telesales team who will start contacting them on behalf of the roofing company.

Pretty smart, eh!

We start with our duties while Mrs Michelle goes back to being 'pre-occupied'. It is almost 3 p.m. and I have gathered about eighty houses while Farah has gathered thirty-five. I ask her if she wants to take a small break and we head out of the office for the fresh, icy cold air.

As we step out, we see Mr Walsh smoking a cigarette. He smiles on seeing us.

Mr Walsh: "Hello, hello! How's your day been so far?"

Farah (sucking up to him): "Hi sir, it's been fine. I am liking to work here."

Mr Walsh: "That's good to hear. Today is a very important day guys. We are expecting a few members from Cool Cola, a very large aerated drinks company to visit us today and we are pitching for their business. If that deal is through, then it's great news for all of us."

We return to our desks. At around 4 p.m., we see Mrs Michelle hurry towards us to tell us that the company representatives of Cool Cola have arrived and will be coming to our section shortly. She tells us to look serious and not interrupt her when she gives them a tour.

We see five people walk in and introduce themselves to Mrs Michelle who introduces us in turn.

Mrs Michelle: "It's great to have you here, guys. We have a super talented team working with us here. We are on our way to change the world and to redefine how sales are done. Why don't you step into my office and let me show you the exciting things we are doing for our clients!"

Ok, this is a completely new person we are seeing. Mrs Michelle is not only being courteous but also praising us and appearing to be this cool, fun person.

We do not see her for the rest of the day. She has apparently left, right after her meeting with the Cool Cola guys.

We complete our target for the day and head home. On my way back home, I am quite happy that at least now, I have a sort of job in an office which isn't so bad. I can see myself working here for at least a year or two.

A few of my college buddies call me up that night to make plans for going clubbing to this club called Tryst. I say, let's do it! We do a bit of pre-drinking along the way and land up at the club to see a long line of people waiting outside.

Me: "Oye Mathew! Isn't today a Monday? By the amount of people here, looks like a weekend!"

Mathew: "I know right! It's some special night tonight, Vishal told me."

Vishal: "Tonight is ladies' night boys! It's gonna be insane!!"

Me: "Hell yea! No wonder I see so many girls here."

We enter Tryst and it is a huge place. Three floors with each floor playing different music. Massive!

Vishal orders for some shots and I hate shots. But he forces me to down them anyway. The club is fairly full and I am buzzed. I order a beer and stand at the bar while Vishal goes dancing and Mathew disappears for a smoke.

I see a group of four girls enter the club and head towards the bar. They order drinks and are talking amongst themselves with their back towards me. I am thinking of talking to the beautiful brunette who looks a little like Emmanuelle Chriqui (Sloan from Entourage series). She suddenly turns towards me and points to my hand.

Girl: "Hi! My friends think you are very cute. What are you drinking?"

Me (thanking my lucky stars): "Hey, I'm drinking beer. Tell your friends, I think you are very cute."

Haha, now that's a pickup line I didn't think I would actually say out loud, but seeing the way she blushed, I guess it worked.

Me: "So, what's your name?"

Girl: "I'm Amanda, that's Jess, Anne and Liz."

Me: "I'm Gaurav. Nice to meet ya'll."

Amanda: "Gaoo?"

Me: "Gau - rav, you gotta roll your tongue for the rav."

Her friends start ordering drinks and Jess and Liz head to the dance floor. Vishal, who is overlooking the entire thing from the dance floor, sees the opportunity and comes over and introduces himself while they are dancing. But he does it in such a creepy manner that the girls suddenly decide to head to the second floor. Vishal, who is sometimes just simply daft to obvious cues, thinks they are inviting him to join on the second floor. Oh well, his bubble is gonna burst soon.

Amanda: "Guurrrav?!"

Me: "Close enough. So, what do you do Amanda?"

Amanda: "I'm studying to become a veterinarian at UofT."

(UofT is the local slang for University of Toronto.)

Me: "Wow, that's pretty cool, I don't know anyone who's studying that. I'm also here for studying. I've just completed my post-grad in Strategic Management at Centennial College."

Amanda: "Your accent is cool, where are you from?"

Me: "I'm from India, Mumbai – the land of Bollywood."

(I don't know why I said the latter part. Haha.)

Amanda: "Hey, I think my friends are calling me upstairs, I'll see you in a bit."

Me: "...."

And she leaves hastily. As if I told her I'm from Afghanistan or something. It does not make any sense and I have to get an answer. But at that moment, my ego is in play and I am like fuck it, I'm here to have a good time and celebrate my new job. So, I down a couple of more beers by the time Mathew arrives.

Me: "Bro, where have you been, smoking since so long?"

Mathew: "No yaar, my parents had called, whenever they call, they speak for a long time. Now, they are saying that they want me to start thinking about marriage. I mean, what the fuck!?"

Mathew bangs the bar counter a little dramatically. I try to calm him down.

Me: "*Koi baat nahi*, don't worry. Here, have a beer. By the way, you won't believe what just happened."

Vishal suddenly comes up to us with a sad face. I guess his bubble has burst. He doesn't say anything but looks at me as if it was my fault.

Me: "Haha, welcome back my shark. How is hunting season?"

Vishal: "Asshole, why did you have to tell her you were Indian. You could have told her you were from South America or something!"

Me: "Whoa! How do you know that? Anyway, what difference does it make? She asked me where I was from and I just said India."

Vishal: "Dude, don't you know, a lot of locals hate Indians. A lot of immigrants from small Indian villages land up here and they misbehave, a lot."

Me: "Haha clearly. I saw how you creepily introduced yourself."

Vishal: "Fuck you! That was unintentional!"

Me: "And you followed them upstairs…"

Vishal: ".... Err I was being friendly! So, Mathew what's up?"

Me: "*Saala*, topic change! Mathew's parents want him to get married"

Vishal: "Hahahaha! Well, that calls for another round of shots!"

We get completely sloshed that night and come out of the club, have an amazing shawarma from a street side joint and head home. An amazing night overall!

I wake up next morning much later than when my alarm first snoozes off, at half past eight. I'm super late.

I take a quick shower, have a bit of cereal and rush for office.

I barely make it by quarter past nine. I am scared that they will fire me for showing up late only on the second day.

I reach the twelfth floor to see a huge number of people waiting outside the office. I locate Farah and go up to her.

Me: "Hey, I thought I was late, what's this commotion?"

Farah: "Gaurav! Come, let's go downstairs."

She looks tensed. We reach downstairs and she asks me for my phone.

Farah: "Can you call the recruitment consultant, who got you this job?"

Me: "Nikos? Sure, but what happened?"

Farah: "First call him."

I dial Nikos's number and his phone is switched off. It keeps going to voicemail. I leave a message asking him to call me back.

Me: "His phone is switched off. I've left a message though."

Farah: "He won't call you back trust me. ***** Professional Services is no longer in business. Turns out, it was set up by this so called Rocket Sales Search Company to hire staff for just a day in order to get that Cool Cola contract. A bogus company sets up a bogus recruitment agency to hire people for a day. Rocket Sales Search wanted to look like a professional set up with a big office and a large team. So that they could pitch for and get the contract. They flew in top execs from all over the country just for a day so that they could bag the deal!"

Me: "Unbelievable! Wow, this is blowing my mind! I guess that was the reason Mrs Michelle was in such a cranky mood."

Farah: "Now that they have the contract, they will outsource the same to some BPO in India for one-tenth the cost."

Me: "I can't believe this is happening! What a sneaky way to do business! Very smart though."

Instead of being angry at them for cheating all the employees, even the Cool Cola Company, I am admiring their bravado and brilliance at the way they have executed the whole thing.

I and Farah hang around for a bit before she leaves. She tells me that she will be moving to Saskatchewan by the end of the winter and that we should stay in touch.

Eventually, everyone leaves that place after shouting expletives and using colourful words since the company has not paid us.

Yet.

Roughly a week later, I receive a cheque at my house address for my services rendered to Rocket Sales Search.

All's well that ends well. Well, almost.

P.S.: Apparently, Mr Walsh is the head of that company and not the guy who is giving the big speech at the beginning of the orientation. Aaah! Mr Walsh, you sneaky s.o.b!

The telephone men

Spring has arrived. The flowers have bloomed. The birds are chirping. No more of that blasted snow! I have seen enough snow since my arrival here to last me a lifetime. Everyone steps out of their houses to become a more outdoorsy culture and the whole city transforms itself. Delicious backyard barbeque aromas are in the air.

My college programme has ended and I am again on my pursuit of finding a good paying job. Everyone from my class is discussing about going to Saskatchewan as it is easier to get a PR (Canadian Permanent Residency) there.

The only catch is you have to work there for about five years in an average temperature of minus three degrees Celsius, as you only receive a provincial PR. It is the local government's way of enticing people to come and work for their state which is highly under populated and lacking quality workforce. Not my cup of tea, I thought.

So, as usual, I continue my job hunt in this beautiful weather. I stumble upon this listing on Craigslist where an American company is looking for a few temporary staff for a contract work at The Park Hyatt in Toronto.

The pay is thirty dollars an hour, which is pretty great. Luckily I get through since I am among the first people to call.

They conduct a short basic interview and tell me to come to The Park Hyatt Hotel after two days at half past six in the morning and they will brief me about the work that needs to be done. It is a three day gig and a ten hour shift.

I reach the Hilton on time. I am greeted by a Mr Rich Simmons who's handling the operations for an American Company called Sinclair Communications. He is assisted by a guy called Ben Haddox.

There are three more guys – Nathan, Ray and Ricky – other than myself who have been assigned to do the job.

Rich comes across as a super warm guy and makes everyone feel comfortable. Ben is the 'fix it guy' who is on the ground with us and will be supervising our work. He's like 'Bob the builder' and has in depth knowledge of almost all hardware things.

We are to reach the storage area of the Park Hyatt which is located on the building's top-most floor to start our duties for the day. Nathan is a talker amongst us and is telling us about his experiences of backpacking across Vietnam, his love for ice hockey and his passion for music. Ray is this good looking, muscular Russian guy whose only aim in life is to 'bang' as many women as possible before he turns forty. He tells us his age is thirty-one and his current fetish is older women. Ask him why and he says, older women are usually sexually dissatisfied and are an easy target. They also foot his bills.

He goes on to tell us that we should join him on his 'jaguar' hunting nights.

Yes, I too didn't know this word until that day.

Jaguars are apparently rich women over the age of fifty and are looking to score younger boys.

Haha.

Yes, many of you might be repulsed by this human being but in his opinion, he is performing a great service by 'helping' those women find happiness.

Ricky is also a character of sorts. He tells us that that he is an 'organic vegan' or something to that effect.

He does not eat meat, most veggies, grains and milk. And oh yes, cooked food also. He shows us an eight-month-old picture of himself and we cannot believe what we see. He was massive. He tells us that his weight then was one hundred and sixty kgs. Since, he has started on this diet of berries and nuts; his weight is now fifty-five kgs.

Wow. Looking at him, we never could have guessed that he used to be so fat, as currently he looks highly malnourished and has bags under his eyes.

In his opinion, he is the healthiest he has ever been. Ok then.

Rich tells us our duties for the day. We have to assemble four thousand phones by 5 p.m.

Four thousand. So, that's a thousand phones each. We have roughly about eight hours, including lunch break.

That's about one hundred and twenty-five phones an hour! Yes, I am just doing the math in my head to make sure I heard him right.

How the heck can one assemble so many phones in such a short time?

As if reading our thoughts, Rich said that it took on an average thirty seconds, even lesser to assemble a phone.

Ben: "Alright guys, here's how you do it. You take the bottom casing of the phone, add the circuit board which clamps on. Next, you connect the phone cord to the circuit board and pass it through the groove at the bottom so that the cord comes out. Now you clamp the top part on, give it a little shake to make sure it is fixed on well and voila!"

The guy did it in less than ten seconds. It seems doable then.

We get started. It seems a bit difficult at first, getting the clamps correctly aligned, but slowly we get the hang of it.

Ray: "Hey Rich, since you are from America, have you been around Toronto?"

Rich: "I've been here twice, but both times, I didn't get much time to go around the city."

Ray: "I would love to show you around boss. I'd take you to this sweet strip club in Downtown where the girls are real nice and they show you a good time."

Rich (sarcastically): "Really, wow. I'd love to but this trip is real short."

Ray: "Come on boss, it will be pretty sweet. We can make time today evening. I'll introduce you to the main girl there. Sweet, sweet ass!"

Rich (now visibly annoyed and ignoring Ray): "So what do you guys do besides temp jobs?"

Ray seems to get the message and shuts up.

Nathan: "I'm pursuing my music, Rich. I'm playing with a band and we mostly practice on weekends. We are trying to land a record deal. Other than that, I love ice hockey. Sucks that Canucks lost against the Bruins. It's not their season this year."

Vancouver Canucks is the ice hockey team of Vancouver which lost the game against Boston Bruins in the 2011 Stanley Cup. Canada, which otherwise is a very peaceful country, becomes quite aggressive when it comes to ice hockey. After the loss, there was a massive riot in downtown Vancouver which was all over the news. A lot of people were injured in that incident and a lot of arrests done by the police.

I don't follow hockey as such but the incident was a chilling reminder of the madness of the fans towards their home team.

Rich: "I am more into NFL, but I had heard about that game. Canucks fans took it pretty hard. What about you Gurave?"

Me (Why can't anyone get my fucking name right!): "It's Gau-RRav. Well, I just completed by studies and I'm applying for full time jobs. Till then, got to pay the rent, so still doing temp jobs in between. Oh, and I also DJ and teach guitar."

Rich: "Gaurave, that's great. Hard work is the essence. Keep at it. What about you Ricky?"

Ricky: "I've recently moved here man. I'm from Ottawa. My girlfriend got a job here, so she asked me to move with her. So, right now I'm in between things. I like this city though, great indie scene."

Ray: "I was working at the oil refineries in Alberta in a small town. It has been three months since I'm back. That town had just one little bar where we could hang in the evenings. I banged the hottest booty there too; she was the wife of the barman."

Ben (As if he hadn't heard what Ray just said): "Guys, let's speed it up a bit. We have to stay on schedule and meet our deadline."

Rich: "Nice to meet you all. I and Ben run Sinclair Communications. Whenever we get a contract, we try to source temporary staff from Craigslist in that city and it's worked out pretty well so far. You seem like a bunch of nice boys. I'll let Ben handle things while I'll be back to check on you guys in a couple of hours."

Ray excuses himself to go downstairs for a smoke. Rich says he'll come along.

We get cracking on those phones. It is monotonous but it gives us room to have a conversation going as we slowly go on autopilot assembling the phones.

Nathan, I and Ricky hit off really well for our love for music. They are mostly into hip hop and trip hop and are telling me about the indie music scene in Toronto.

Both of them are trying to pursue a career in the music industry in Toronto – Ricky trying to get live gigs to play in various pubs and clubs in and around GTA while Nathan trying to land a record deal. It's things like this that make me wonder the passion which people have to pursue their dreams and the sacrifices they make along the way. Unlike India, earning a buck or two in Toronto is relatively easier if you do temporary jobs, at least you can earn a decent wage and afford basic amenities as the inflation in Canada is not as high as in India and things are mostly cheap here, including rent. (Provided you do not convert everything to Indian rupees. Newbie NRIs have this bad 'ancestral trait' of converting everything to rupees when living abroad. A dollar when you convert directly is almost sixty rupees, but if you are earning there and spending there itself, its equivalent conversion is hardly about fifteen rupees because that is how much it is worth when you see the price of things and how many dollars you are earning on an average.)

By lunch time, we have almost done six hundred phones each. Even Ray, who surprised me, because of the amount of crap the guy talked, when it comes to work, he delivers. We are instructed to go to the Hyatt staff kitchen to have our lunch.

We stuff our faces with the delicious spread in the staff kitchen. It is almost like a mini buffet with salad, steak, couscous, hash browns, soup and pasta and soufflé for desert. Yum!

I have never had couscous before and it is amazing. It's a bit like *sabudana khichdi* but with a slightly meatier flavour because it's cooked in meat broth.

Rich and Ben also join us a little while later and have very little to eat and mostly coffee. Rich tells us, that they have some good news for us.

Rich: "Guys, you have done some really great work. We have assembled a total of twenty three hundred phones. I just had a word with the hotel management and I have some good news. We don't have to assemble any more phones as they said that they only need about twenty-two hundred of them. So, it looks like we will be starting installation of those phones from here on. Also, don't worry about the hours. We will pay you as promised."

We are very relieved to hear the great news. No more assembling!

Ben: "Yeah people, looks like you guys caught a lucky streak! Let's proceed to the first floor of the hotel, from there we will start installing those phones in the rooms. Rich will be in the room service office to check if each of our phone is installed and working correctly."

Rich: "Ricky, come with me. Both of us will be on phone duty to check if we completed the installations correctly. Alright guys, one more thing. Please keep your voices down as we do not want to disturb the residents of the rooms. Thanks!"

We reach the first floor of the hotel to start our installations. Ben introduces us to Allen, who is a house-keeping executive and has the master key to open the rooms. Allen looks bored as hell and hardly speaks except when issuing instructions. He knocks twice to make sure there is no one in the room. Then he uses his master key to open that room.

Ben: "Ok people, let's split into teams. Allen will keep opening rooms and we will enter, install, check and wait for Rich to call us in the room and then leave. Ray, you come with me. Nathan and Gurive can work together. Kapeesh?"

Nathan: "Yes, boss!"

Me (Thinking if I should change my name to Garry or something): "Sure, Ben."

We enter the room, unplug the existing phone cord from the wall clamp and remove the phone instrument and plug in our new phone. Either Rich or Ricky calls us to check if the phone is working fine. We follow the same protocol for every room.

First three floors are completed smoothly and quite fast. We take roughly five minutes for each room. On the fourth floor, I and Nathan start with one of the presidential suites. It is a massive two-storied room. Allen knocks on the door to check if anyone is inside.

Unlocking the door, we step inside to what I can describe as ultimate luxury. There is a giant chandelier bang in the centre of the room above a grand piano which looks spotless and shiny. There is a balcony area, a large living room, a smaller room downstairs and a master bedroom upstairs. Someone is already occupying this room as we can see a huge pile of belongings, suitcases and what not.

Nathan starts with the living room and I go up to the master bedroom. I plug in the new phone set near the bedside.

Then, I am informed by Ben that there is another one in the bathroom. I enter the bathroom which too is ginormous. I remove the wall phone next to the mirror when I feel something crawling up my leg. I look down and see nothing. I walk towards the bed, where the new phone set is kept and come back to plug it in the bathroom. I am admiring the beautiful artwork around the mirror and check out my reflection while waiting for Rich to call me on the new phone. I see another face checking itself out with me. It is on my shoulder next to my ear and is looking straight in the mirror. And oh yes, it is a lime green coloured snake.

Yes, you read that right.

A fucking snake.

In a suite.

On my shoulder. Looking at itself.

Don't move an inch, Gaurav, don't even twitch, I think. My mind is scrambling for ways to escape this odd-scary scenario when another entity is added to our reflection. A beautiful girl enters the bathroom and scrambles towards me. Despite my scenario, I can't help notice her extremely low cut top and her exquisite smelling perfume.

She seems to be telling me something. But, I am not listening. I am battling a near death scenario and a hard-on.

Hot girl: "Pooki baby! Sorry baby, don't be scared. Mommy's here now. Don't worry guy, he's harmless."

Pooki? FUCKING POOKI!

Here, I am in this dangerous situation and the stupid bitch is apologizing to her snake. I mean, what the fuck!

She strokes its neck and the snake turns towards her. Then, she gently picks him up and takes him to a fish tank like thing.

Hot/Crazy girl: "Hi, he's all well now. Sorry about that. He does that sometimes. But don't worry, he's not poisonous. Snowy is, but he's back home. We keep him locked up at all times. I love reptiles, snakes in particular. They are so graceful. Also, here's two hundred bucks, please don't tell anyone at the hotel as I have sneaked him in. They do not allow them here."

Ok, this is a new breed of psycho-carrying your pet snake when going on vacation. I have heard of dogs and cats, but this is a first. A snake called Pooki. And another one called Snowy.

Kya bakchodi hai!

Nathan is done with the ground area of the suite and is chatting with Ben waiting for me when I come down with a dazed look on my face and $200 in my pocket. Shock and glee in my heart at the same time.

Ben: "Yeah, I know Guriv, she's smoking. She just came back to get something from her bathroom."

Nathan: "What took you so long bro? She's hot eh!"

Me: "Huh? Yes... err... phone's working fine."

Nathan: "You ok dude? You look a little dazed."

Me: "Yes, I'm fine. Just a little thirsty. Ben, can we take a short break?"

Ben: "Sure guys, see you in fifteen."

Me and Nathan, head downstairs to the staff kitchen.

Nathan: "Ok, spit it out. What the heck happened upstairs?"

I narrate to him the weird chain of events in the bathroom and he is laughing his ass off.

Me: "And to top it off, she gave me two hundred bucks. Don't discuss it with anyone here though as the hotel management might find out."

Nathan: "Hahahaaha, don't worry, but that is one heck of a scene. I mean, I can't imagine myself feeling afraid and having a hard on at the same time! Hahahahhahaha!"

Me: "Fucker! I was literally shitting my pants. And yes, she was hot. For some reason, I wanted her, then and there itself! Crazy huh!"

Nathan (guffawing): "The crazier they are, the hotter they seem. Looks like you got paid son!"

Ray and Ricky join us. Ray is looking a little pissed off. Ricky looks a little tense also.

Me: "What's up? Is everything alright?

Ray doesn't reply. He is staring at the floor.

Ricky: "He's been through a lot man. Let the man be."

Nathan: "Been through what?"

Ricky: "It was at one of the rooms on the fifth floor. We entered the room and went on to plug in the new sets. Ray went to the bathroom and I heard him shout, angrily swearing his heart out. Turns out, his girlfriend was staying in that room with some other dude. I didn't know he had a girlfriend. Poor guy is crushed. Her phone's switched off too."

Me: "There is something about the bathrooms in this hotel! So, how did he know it was his girlfriend?"

Ray suddenly gets up to remove something from the back pocket of his jeans. It is a small bracelet.

On closer inspection, we see that it has the following text engraved on it:

Ty takaya krasivaya...

– Ray

Ray: "I gave this to her. It means 'you are so beautiful' in Russian."

All of us are silent now. We feel bad for the guy. I mean, who would have thought that this jaguar hunter had a sensitive side as well for all the general crap that comes out of his mouth. Sure, he too must be two-timing, even ten-timing her, but I don't know why but I feel a little sorry for him.

The rest of the day passes without much incident. We managed to complete all installations by half past six in the evening. Rich is very pleased with the work done and tells us that the hotel management is very happy with how swiftly and quietly we complete our work without disturbing the residents. He and Ben are also staying at the same hotel and invite us for a few beers in his room.

Ray says that he has to be somewhere and will not be joining us. He takes his money and leaves without a word. I, Ricky and Nathan hang around for another couple hours having beers, onion rings and poutine which Rich has ordered. During that time, Ben is mostly on the phone talking to his kids while Rich is telling us about his hometown back home in the US.

I make the guys watch a few epic Rajnikanth scenes on YouTube which have the guys rolling on the floor laughing. Even Ben disconnects his call to watch the madness. He even makes a note of the names of movies telling us that he wants to show this to his kids.

P.S.: I run into that hot/crazy girl again in the lobby of the hotel that night. I am getting out of the elevator while she is getting in. She smiles and gives me a slap on my butt.

Enough said.

Animal instincts

We are into the second semester of our post-grad programme. Days move more swiftly as we are bogged down with a lot of assignments and term work. The grading system is such that 50% is based on the assignments done by you throughout the semester and the rest is your performance during the exams. For me, studies are a priority, and I am doing pretty well. Even though I would be out doing temp jobs, I make sure that I complete my assignments and studies on time. Being out of my comfort zone, doing different kinds of jobs really teaches one the concept of humility and independence. One thing I feel that Indians are lagging behind in is that we instantly judge a person based on their class or economic status. We prefer to be comfortable with people of our own class and aspire to move up a class.

Well, we are a developing country anyway, so I guess class competitiveness is another factor of herd mentality. I do not blame the people though. A lot of Indian newspapers (biggest ones) are responsible for this shift of focus from judging a person based on their character to judging them based on class. You must remember the times when the job placement salaries of IIMs were shown and celebrated in newspapers. Those articles were there almost on a daily basis, showing students, fresh out of college, getting starting salaries of tens of lakhs of rupees per year. This in turn bought a seismic shift in mindsets of many, parents especially, who pressured their children to make it or break it in order to be 'happy' and lead a better life. So, the entire country aspired to be after the golden carrot which only a select few managed to grab.

Anyway, so back in Canada, I notice that even though people value their personal space a lot, they would seldom change their behaviour when speaking to a person of lower class. After the mid-term exams, we have about two weeks off after which the last part of our semester would begin. I, Vishal, Shirish and Mathew decide to take a road trip across Canada crossing four states up to Banff National Park.

After mapping out the road, Vishal and Shirish leave for the rental car agency to pick out a car for our trip. Me and Mathew are just sitting at home, playing computer games, waiting for them to return.

An hour later, my phone rings and it's Vishal calling.

Vishal: "Broooooo! Come downstairs ASAP!"

Me: "Why, what happened?"

Vishal: "You won't believe which car we got!"

Excited, Mathew and I rush downstairs. On reaching our building parking lot, we see Vishal and Shirish standing next to a beast.

Whoa! I cannot believe what I see! It's a Dodge Charger!

I have been a car fanatic since birth and this is one epic car, I must say. V6 engine and about two hundred and ninety horses under the hood. This is a thing of beauty. They get the car really cheap as some last minute deal was on.

Our road trip is gonna be so kickass! For our trip, we have bought sleeping bags and tents as we are planning on doing a bit of camping also. Shirish has come up with an awesome *jugaad* to get our tents and sleeping bags for free. He suggested we buy the same from Walmart which has a thirty days return policy. So, once we are back from our trip, we can return them and get our money back, no questions asked.

Jugaad ftw!

It is almost 11 in the morning by the time we leave. Toronto to Banff is almost thirty-five hundred kms. So, we will be crossing Ontario, Manitoba, Saskatchewan into the state of Alberta.

It is almost the distance from Kashmir to Kanyakumari. And we will be doing that twice. We stuff our bags in the trunk and head out into the horizon. Highways here are a thing of beauty. Our beast eats up kilometres quickly and by lunch time, we have almost reached midway across our state of Ontario. (Notice I said kilometres and not miles because Canada too follows the British metric system and not the American one.)

We stop over at a McDonalds' for a super yummy cheeseburger lunch. Stuffing our faces with the fare, we pocket at least twenty to thirty packets of hot sauce, ketchup and tissues, since we figure we might need them during our camping expedition.

We are back on the road after our quick lunch so that we cover up as much distance as possible during daylight. The temperature slowly starts to drop as evening draws closer. As we close in on the edge of Ontario State, we are in sort of a no man's zone where even small convenience stores are few and far between. It is about 7 p.m. and we can still see bright daylight as though it is daytime. We decide to keep driving till we see it getting darker and then find a place to camp out for the night.

Summer has not yet started as it is still the middle of spring and the weather is still relatively colder with a lot of wind chill. All of us are equally surprised and fascinated with this weather phenomenon seeing such bright daylight in the evening. Time passes quickly as we play a lot of dumb charades and indulging in our favourite past time, 'taking each other's cases'. It's funny how much time can be spent just mimicking someone's idiosyncrasies.

Mathew or Shirish are usually the *bakras*, ending up under mine or Vishal's crosshairs.

Mathew is this heavy set Mallu-Catholic guy who was doing a cushy high paid job as a relationship manager at Citibank in Dubai when he decided to study further to break the monotony and experience a new country. Hence, Canada happened.

During his first month here, there was a student welcoming party on campus. At the party, someone dared a guy called Raymond to jump from the first floor of the building.

Mathew, in his highly inebriated state thought that it was a hazing ceremony, i.e. a college initiation ritual to 'welcome' new joinees – similar to ragging in India.

Yes, I know, drunken people can be so stupid.

While the other guy chickened out at the last minute, Mathew shouted *Vande Mataram* and jumped! And Humpty Dumpty had a great fall.

He broke his leg and passed out on the ground and we had to call the ambulance to rush him to the hospital. This incident made Mathew somewhat of a legend in college. And this is the incident which has us laughing our asses off every time we recall it. We love imitating Mathew in his moment of glory or downfall, as we say.

Vande Mataram!

Mathew says that he enjoyed his stint at the hospital quite a bit because he was really pampered by the nurse taking care of him.

And, oh, was she hot! We tease him, that every time she came in, Mathew would put a pillow over his crotch to hide his boner!

I cannot help but marvel at the beauty that the countryside keeps throwing at us. It is to be seen to be believed. I mean, it is like we are tripping on picturesque landscape, our minds completely mesmerized.

Daylight refuses to abandon us as it is nearly 9 p.m. and we are still driving. After Ontario ends, the state of Manitoba begins. We are passing through a long winding road surrounded by tall trees, on both sides, making the sky nearly invisible. Streaks of sunlight can be seen creeping in through the gaps of the trees, making it a sight to experience.

Natural beauty truly is the forte of Canada!

Vishal sees a remote little store about to close for the day and suggests we make a pit stop. The store is more of a souvenir and snack shop selling little trinkets and stuff for tourists.

The owner, Dennis is a huge guy with a moustache and has like a permanent frown on his face. He speaks very little except asking us where we are driving to. He is surprised to hear that we are driving from Toronto to Banff this time of the year and even more shocked to hear that we are Indians. He has never heard of a bunch of Indian boys driving all the way. So, in a way, it's a first for all of us.

His store has authentic coonskin caps which I have always wanted to see since a long time. (A coonskin cap is made of the skin and fur of a raccoon and is worn by people living in colder regions. Also, it was somewhat of a fad in the 1950s when it made its way to high fashion.)

It looks like one of those furry Nehru *topis* that Kashmiris wear with a raccoon's tail at the end of it.

They are ridiculously expensive here but there is no harm in clicking a picture wearing it. We look like idiots posing with those caps together, but hey, who cares!

We grab sausages, marshmallows and a bit of other grub which we will be roasting on our camp fire. Provided we find a camp site.

Dennis wishes us safe travel and we are back on the road again. We are looking for a RV camping park site where we can camp for the night. The sun is finally starting to set on us as it nears half past ten. All of us are now getting frustrated as there is no campsite in sight. We decide that we will take the next turn whichever comes first and just park in that lane and spend the night in the car.

Soon enough, a small right turn comes up, going into a tiny little road. We head into that tiny road which has room enough for only our car.

We keep driving up that road in complete silence when suddenly a woman's voice breaks the silence scaring us to bits.

"Turn around."

"You have diverted from your original route."

"Turn around."

Turns out it was our GPS telling us that we have ventured off course.

Haha.

We pass by a huge bungalow-like house with a massive backyard which might be someone's holiday home. Soon, that road ends. We realize this might be a private road. It is slowly getting darker and we cannot head back on the road again.

Shirish suggests that we camp in the backyard of the house.

With no other option, we agree.

Vishal and I scout the backyard for where we can set up camp. Mathew and Shirish unload the tents and other stuff from the boot. I find a spot where someone might have lit a camp fire. There are rocks neatly laid in a circle on the ground and at the centre of the circle are the remains of ash from the last fire. It is nearly dark now as it is past 11 p.m. and the sun has set on us.

Sunset at 11 p.m. – only in Canada. Well, other countries also, but I haven't visited any of them. So, first things first. To set up a tent. And no one knows how.

While the rest of the guys are trying to figure that out, I decide to start a fire.

I gather a few fallen branches, leaves and make a large pile within the circle. I make a tiny pile to start a fire from which then I will transfer it to the large one. There is only one problem – all the wood is damp. I decide to light up stuff that will catch fire faster and then transfer that to the damp wood.

I grab like twenty to thirty tissues from the car and pile them up and light them on fire. Not my brightest moment. The flame consumes those flimsy tissues within seconds and I am back to square one. It has been almost forty minutes since we have been trying to set up a tent and light a fire. Neither venture successful.

Then I have a brainwave. The outer portion of the tree might be damp due to the weather, but the inner portion should be dry. And the wood on these trees is quite soft that it can be peeled off by hand.

As I have thought, the wood inside is very dry. Scraping as many wood shavings as possible from the tree, I place them on my smaller pile and light the match. Soon enough, the thing lights up!

Eureka! We have fire!

Man has created fire. From the elements, going back to our ancestors.

As King Leonidas of '*300*' said, "Spartans! Prepare for glory!"

Ok, I'll shut up. Super excited I am though to have done that.

Meanwhile, these guys also manage to set up a dangly looking tent which at least stands upright for us to get in.

Right, so let the games begin!

We have carried booze from our favourite LCBO store in Toronto. (LCBO stands for the Liquor Control Board of Ontario and it is the Canadian equivalent of a *theka* or a wine shop.)

Sipping our favourite Jack Daniels by the campfire in the cool air whilst munching on fire-roasted sausages and marshmallows, needless to say is one of the best nights of my life.

One by one, each one of us gets crazy drunk and starts dancing around the fire. Shirish says that he's had enough for the day as he has been driving most of the time and retires to the tent.

Vishal: "Boys! This is so amazing!! And I'm so druuuuunnkkk!"

Mathew: "*Jinke sar ho ishq ki chhaao…paao ke neeche jannat hooogiii. Jinke sar ho ishhhq kiiiii chhaooooooo!*

Chal chhaiiya chhaiiya chhaiiyaa chhaiiyaaa!"

We all start singing. Impromptu!

We can hear Shirish join in from the background whilst lying down in the tent.

This goes on for about ten songs when Vishal decides he wants to explore the house.

We convince him to explore the area instead of the house, lest we get arrested. Well, technically we are already trespassing. We walk a little away from the campsite towards the woods. Mathew takes the lead while I and Vishal have now switched to drinking beer and are trying to open a can while walking.

After about five minutes, we see Mathew disappear in front of us as though he fell through a hole. We run towards his direction to fall down ourselves, down a small sandy slope. The sand is soft as velvet and shiny in the night sky.

We have discovered a beach! It is one of those moments which completely take you by surprise. A beautiful little beach across a lake. (First I thought it was the sea, and then as though echoing my thoughts, Vishal suggested that it might be a lake since we are in a landlocked area.)

The water was still and crystal clear, reflecting the starry sky above – our little piece of heaven.

We sat there in silence, taking in the magnificence of the surroundings.

Mathew: "Fuck, this is amazing. And this is the second fucking time I have fallen after I'm drunk when I am around you guys!"

Me: "Hahahaha! You have now successfully completed level one of the initiation ceremony! Now, for level two, you have to run naked through the campus and...."

Mathew: "Basssstarrrrd!"

Vishal (Blissfully unaware and on his own trip): Baby, I miss you too, come *na* fast. Mathew, you are a nice guy but why do you fall so much? Gaurav, remember that party you played at a pub called Chikoroo? I am hungry…"

And he passes out on the sand.

Face down.

I and Mathew burst out into uncontrollable laughter, which lasts for about fifteen minutes. We finish the rest of the beer, have a couple more, pick up Vishal and head back to the camp site. On reaching our tent, we see Shirish's feet jutting out from the tent entrance. We place Vishal next to him; I squeeze inside and so does Mathew. We are quite hammered at this point, so the nice comfy sleeping bag is like an old friend.

We also fall asleep (pass out) in literally two seconds.

The sky is crimson. The air is filled with acrid smog. The battle is on with all guns blazing.

Vishal: "Let's dig a tunnel under these assholes and come out from the other side!"

Me: "But how will only the two of us manage to dig all the way? It's almost two kilometres!"

Mathew: "Vandeeee Matarammm!! *Inn bhosdiwaalo ki gaand maar denge*!! I will dig hundred kilometres under their ass and blow them to smitherrrrreeeeeennnnnssss!"

For some reason, he was swearing like a Delhiite.

Mathew starts digging frantically and within moments, vanishes underground.

Me: "I cannot move guys! I think I'm on a landmine!"

Vishal: "You can do this Gaurav, one swift movement. I'll pull you towards safety!"

Me: "Noooooo, don't! You go ahead, I will defend from here!"

Vishal (pulling my hands): "We won't leave you behind. We will win this!!"

Me (pushing him away, kicking him): "Go Vishal, you will be in danger also. I will cover you! Gooooooooo!"

Suddenly, I feel a slap across my face. I wake up in a daze. I see Vishal standing over me shouting something. I feel like he's telling me something. My mind cannot focus. Need to understand his language.

Vishal: "Wake up fucckerr! Wake the fuck up!"

I suddenly sit up, my eyes fully red, but alert. I can hear that it's raining heavily. Although I am dry. I see a guy sitting on Mathew's stomach trying to wake him. Mathew is completely drenched from his head till his chest. I realize I'm in our tent. The guy trying to wake Mathew is Shirish. Mathew slept with his head outside the tent entrance and his legs inside the tent when he passed out last night. Because of the rain, he is now fully drenched, but still passed out. Vishal, on seeing me awake, diverts his attention to Mathew and gives him a hard slap across his face also. Mathew springs out of sleep and in panic stands and runs out of the tent. A tree appears out of nowhere and he dashes his head into it.

He is now sitting there, equally dazed and confused as to what the fuck is going on.

Shirish: "How much did you fuckers drink last night? I have been trying to wake you since half an hour."

Vishal: "Gaurav, what the heck! You kicked me in my stomach."

Shirish: "We have to pack up ASAP because these tents will be ruined in this kind of rain and then we won't be able to return them to Walmart. Come on, let's hurry!"

Me (finally able to comprehend what is happening): "Sorry Vishal, weird dream. Let's pack!"

We scramble around and manage to get all our stuff, pack it and stuff it in the boot of the car. Mathew watches from a distance, still sitting under that tree. We rush back to get Mathew on his feet into the car. Finally, we are sitting in the car, Shirish in the driver's seat, Mathew going shotgun, I and Vishal at the back. Mathew passes out again in the front. All of us too fall asleep after discussing our next POA (plan of action) for the day. Just before sleeping, I check my phone to see the time.

It was quarter to six in the morning. I wake up to see the car empty.

No wait! Mathew is still sleeping in the front seat. We are parked outside some diner. I step out of the car to stretch my legs and check the time.

11 a.m.

A few moments later, I see Shirish and Vishal walking back towards the car with some food packed for us. We keep the food on the boot of the car and have our breakfast. It is chicken sandwiches, pancakes and coffee. Bliss!

I don't have much of a hangover but the same cannot be said for Mathew. After about twenty minutes, he too, groggily steps out of the car. He wolfs down his breakfast cursing us that we are the reason he bumped his head into that tree and we are guffawing again. It's funny how someone's misery can be so hilarious.

We recall the scenario from last night and today morning and I tell the others about my battlefield dream. Vishal frowns. Coincidentally, Mathew too was having a similar dream of being on a battlefield. What are the odds!

Anyway, so we are back on the road again. We decide to keep driving till we cross the state of Manitoba into Saskatchewan. As we enter the state of Saskatchewan, we can see signs everywhere on the highway telling us to drive cautiously as there might be animals like deer, and moose trying to cross the road.

It starts to rain a little when we are about to cross the city of Regina, around 4 p.m. It is the first time I have heard that name, so, sitting in the car and nothing to do, we make childish jokes about the name of the city which rhymes with a certain part of the female anatomy. Some of the jokes are super hilarious at that time, although now I cannot recall even a single one.

The sun has already set (at 4 p.m.?) and the weather is quite cold, about four degrees, which is warm by Canadian standards. The rain, I guess, is making it colder. We decide to drive on till we reach the city of Calgary which is in Alberta, which we predict should take about five more hours.

The rain has now reached a torrential downpour, forcing us to slow down. Mathew is now driving and Shirish is sitting in front with him with me and Vishal at the back as usual. We are driving at about a hundred km/hr when suddenly I am jolted forward and smack my nose behind Shirish's seat. Vishal and Shirish too smack their heads into whatever is in front of them. Mathew has slammed on the brakes hard due to something he sees on the road in front of us. The mighty Dodge Charger fishtails and screeches to a halt inches before something that has caused us to stop in the first place.

We cannot believe what we see in front of us.

It is a MOOSE!

I had never seen one in my life, so seeing one up so close is something which I can never forget.

The animal was huge!

I mean, really bigger than I have imagined.

Had we run into it, our car would have totaled completely. It is at least six feet in height and has huge antlers five feet across. I figure it must be a male because only male moose grow antlers and females do not. All of us sit there in silence as the magnificent creature slowly trots across the road.

It stops right in front of our car and makes like a loud rumbling sound looking right at us. Our hearts are in our mouths not knowing what to do. Then, he turns around and continues on his way.

As soon as he left, Mathew accelerates fast lest it turns back. As the car pulls away, we turn back to see the mighty creature disappear into the woods on the other side of the road. Coming face to face with that magnificent animal is something which gives me goose bumps to this day.

The rest of the journey to Calgary is mostly uneventful.

We stop by at a Hooters pub though. For the unaware, Hooters is a place to kick back a few beers and savour their hot and tasty food served by even hotter waitresses wearing hot shorts and crop tops.

Our jaws literally drop open seeing the bevy of beauties trotting about the place because they are really gorgeous.

We have a beer or two each, just for the experience of Hooters.

We are famished as our last meal was in the afternoon, but we decide that we will eat once we reach Calgary after checking into a hotel.

We finally reach Calgary by 11 p.m. We get a good last minute deal at a hotel with a nice room and comfy beds. So, it is good to have a proper bed to sleep on, especially after last night's madness.

But our stomachs are rumbling.

We decide to head down to the restaurant inside the hotel, hoping that it is still open and we can eat.

The restaurant is closed with one Chinese guy cleaning the tables.

Me: "Excuse me, can we order food now or have it to go please?"

Chinese Waiter Guy: "*Noohi bhoiiyyaa, khaana bund.*"

Oo teri! So the guy was not Chinese, Nepali maybe then, going by his accent.

Me: "*Bhai*, please *kuch jugaad kar de, bahut door se aaye hain hum.* Toronto *se.*"

Nepali Waiter Guy: "Toronto! *Waah bhoiiyyaa, main pauuch saal pihele Gerrard Strit pe eak hotal pe kom kiya!*"

Gerrard Street is majorly an Indian/Bangladeshi dominated area of Toronto. It is literally like a typical dirty Indian street having you-name-it-they-have-it type of Indian food/drink/ *paan*/etc. They even have our Indian cigarettes there.

Me: "*Acha! Badiya hai yaar woh jagah! Main uske paas hi rehta hoon.*"

I live in Scarborough which is quite far from the area, but I am trying to appeal to a man to give us some food!

Nepali Waiter Guy: "*Boooht chooothiya jogaah hai bhoiiyya! Main isiliye yohaan aa goya!*"

All the guys are cracking up. I cannot control my laughter also, but my focus is food. Hence, I press on.

Me: "*Dekh, tu khaana khila de, hum tujhe thoda extra de denge. Bill bhi mat banana.*"

I slide him twenty bucks, seeing which his eyes light up. Hahaa, works like a charm, whatever the country!

Nepali Waiter Guy (pointing to a table near the kitchen): "*Oaap log voo table pi bithoo. Maii leke aata hoon.*"

He first goes towards the restaurant door to close it and lock it from inside. Then he smiles at us and goes towards the kitchen. All the boys are praising me for my negotiating skills while we are waiting for the meal to arrive. We hope at least the guy can whip up some leftovers for us to eat. The guy seems to be taking his own sweet time.

We pass time by watching our photos from the previous night and during the day. It feels great to have those moments captured on camera.

Still, we keep looking at the time as we are super famished.

Finally, a good forty-five minutes later, he appears holding a tray in his hand. He places it on the table and disappears back into the kitchen. Comes back two seconds later holding another tray.

And another.

And another!

Wow, the guy has set up a mini buffet for us!

We see the following items in front of us:

Chicken Tikka Masala

Paneer Bhurji

Daal Tadka

Chole Masala

Butter Tandoori Rotis

Lassi

Suji ka Halwa

This is what heaven looks like. All of us cheer and hug him when we see this.

The food not only looks good, but tastes amazing. Turns out, he is the cook and is cleaning the tables today as the waiters had to leave early.

I haven't had such amazing Punjabi food even in India. I mean seriously, the guy has mad skills.

He also sits down across us to give us company. We narrate him our antics from the night before and he cracks up. We are thoroughly enjoying every bite of our godsent food.

After licking our plates clean, we thank him again, tip him another 20 and head for our rooms to catch our forty winks. Tomorrow, we have to drive only about one hundred and thirty kilometres to reach Banff National Park which should take us an hour and a half maximum.

We leave Calgary at ten in the morning, after having a good night's sleep. The Banff National Park is massive and is a place one must visit at least once in their lifetime. The sheer natural beauty is unparallel. You can camp, trek, cycle, ride a cable car, enjoy a dip in a hot sulphur spring as well as see the various flora and fauna which you might not have seen before. Basically, you can experience all the wonderful things our mother earth has to offer.

I have never seen a Bighorn Sheep aka Ram in my life. Only heard about it.

It is a beautiful intimidating animal with its horns curling downwards looking like a 'curly letter M' on its head.

It is also the logo of the automobile company Dodge.

While inside the park, a huge herd of rams pass us on one of the internal roads inside the park.

It is like we are waiting at a traffic signal waiting for the other vehicles to pass.

After driving around the park for a while, we find this beautiful spot next to the Bow River which flows through the centre of the park. We had packed a few sandwiches from a restaurant nearby and a few apple ciders (*obviously*).

Parking our car next to the river, we just sit there for a while, absorbing in the breathtaking views.

Vishal plays 'Stairway to heaven' on the car stereo. Led Zepplin has been one of my all time favourite bands since my engineering days, when I was exposed to the magic of rock and heavy metal. Every syllable that Robert Plant says goes in sync with our collective emotions at that point in time as we have reached this heaven on earth sort of place concluding our wonderful road trip.

Just when the lead of the song is about to start, I see something moving upriver about a kilometre away, playing in the water.

Me (pointing towards the object in the river): "Mathew! What is that?"

Mathew (squinting his eyes): "I don't know. Looks like a crocodile."

Shirish (guffawing): "What the fuck would a crocodile be doing here?"

Me: "I think it is swimming towards us."

Soon enough, the 'object' starts to move down the river towards the spot where we are sitting.

Vishal (standing on the bonnet of the car, Mathew also joining him): Fuckkk! I hope it's not what you are saying or I'll kill you Mathew!"

Me: "Hahaha *fattu saale*. I am sure it is not a bloody crocodile!"

Now, the 'object' is only half a kilometre away, it starts to take shape and we see what it really is.

It is a large duck.

All of us burst out laughing, except Mathew. He is still on the bonnet of the car.

So, the duck swims to our spot and comes out of the water quacking loudly.

Mathew moves from the bonnet to the roof of the car.

Seeing the sandwiches lying open on the grass, the duck rushes towards one with lightening speed. Before we can react, it has half a sandwich in its mouth. Then, it comes next to us unafraid and keeps the sandwich on the ground and starts eating piece by piece. Unbelievable!

So, here we are listening to Led Zep whilst eating sandwiches, drinking ciders and having a duck join us for lunch.

And Mathew sitting on the roof of the car, petrified.

Who would have 'thunk' it!

We stay in Banff for another day exploring the place, meeting locals and have a grand time.

The day after, we bid goodbye to the incredible place. We plan to drive almost non-stop throughout till Toronto because the last date for returning our rental car is almost here and we have to cover a lot of ground.

We decide to take turns so that we keep driving for at least eighteen to nineteen hours a day. We calculate we should reach Toronto within two days, flat.

On our first day, we cover a lot of distance, nearly twenty-three hundred kilometres, as we enter Manitoba. It is almost midnight. We park the car on the side of the road where there is a large patch of trees and sleep for a few hours before one of us starts driving again. It is Shirish's turn to drive in the morning, 4 a.m. onwards.

I am the first one to fall asleep as I am exhausted from the long ride. I am also the first one to wake up. Rubbing my eyes, I check my watch to see the time.

It is 9 a.m. We overslept and how!

I step out of the car to stretch my legs.

There is a van parked about thirty feet ahead of us with the letters 'Nat Geo' written on it.

Sleepily, I think, Nat Geo... Nat Geo... National Geographic!

Visibly excited, I am now wide awake as I rush back to the car to wake the others.

Me (pointing towards the van): "Wake up guys! Look!"

Every one of them echoes my excitement on seeing the van.

Vishal: "Holllly crappp! A National Geographic van parked right in front of us!"

Mathew: "There must be an animal close by, which they must be shooting!"

Shirish: "Gaurav, come back inside the car. It will be safer from here if that animal is dangerous."

Judging by our 'moose' experience, I do not want to take any chances and I am back in the car.

Shirish starts the car and slowly inches it forward to move ahead of the parked van in order to locate where the Nat Geo folks might be shooting.

We see a few cars behind us also slow down and park on the side of the road. Clearly, they also must have seen the van.

People are now stepping out of their cars to take a closer look.

We too gather the courage to step out and see what the fuss is all about.

Soon, we encounter the crew a little deeper in the foliage sitting deathly still with their camera pointing towards an animal. That animal happens to be a large black bear rubbing its back on one of the tree barks. I have now seen it all.

There is a small crowd beside us gazing at the bear who is clearly now a star.

Snapping pictures, people are chatting excitedly amongst one another.

Suddenly, we see the bear stop whatever it is doing, and stand deathly still. It turns its head towards us, looking menacing. Without warning, the bear charges in our direction. It is fear and death staring us straight in the face.

Panicking, everyone runs back to their cars. The boys have already reached the car while I and Shirish are lagging behind. To run faster, I remove my flip flops and leave them behind to run at full speed towards our car. We shut our doors and lock our windows. The bear comes out from the trees, charging. About ten feet away from our cars, the bear abruptly changes direction to cross the road and head towards the trees on the other side.

Phew! That was a close call. Had any one of us been outside, one swipe of the mighty bear's paw would have been instant death.

We quickly start our car and make the last leg of our journey hoping we do not run into any more animals!

We enter Toronto that night from what has been a stupendous trip of a lifetime.

We camped at someone else's property, almost crashed into a moose, had the most delicious Punjabi food cooked by a Nepali cook, dined with a duck which was not on our plate and almost had a 'bear hug'.

P.S.: Coincidentally, guess what is the name of the place in Saskatchewan where we almost crashed our car into a moose? *Moose Jaw.*

Little ol' lady in a big Red house

∞

There once was a little old lady who lived in a big red house. All alone she lived in her home with no one for company but a stray ol' mouse.

Winter was nigh, snow piled up on her driveway so high. With no one to help, she prayed for a miracle from up high.

Her little shovel was hardly any good, turned away the few who came to help her, but they hardly could.

There once was an Indian boy who passed by her lane, saw her pale face sitting by the window pane.

He thought that she needed help, seeing the amount of snow. Ran back to get his friends to help out with her woe.

Her eyes lit up seeing so many folks, her little heart thanked that tall Indian bloke.

An hour passed, then two. Seeing such enthusiasm, the snow started to shoo.

Before long, her driveway was as good as new. She stepped out with a plate full of goodies to feed her heroic crew.

She hugged each one, the Indian bloke extra tight, for he was her saviour, her shining knight.

P.S.: I always wanted to write an ode about the little ol' lady in her big red abode.

Salvageable or Non-salvageable?

One of my cousins from Delhi wanted to marry via the arranged route. So at the time, she is in touch with a prospective groom. That's how I meet Brijesh. He is that prospective groom's best friend who lives in Toronto.

While they do not end up marrying, I and Brijesh hit off really well.

I meet him at a point in my life when I am still trying to figure out what exactly I want to do. Yes, I have done a lot of part time/odd jobs, but still, I am looking for something that would really ignite the passion inside me that would make me want to get out of bed every day and give my best.

Brijesh is, in the true sense of the word, a hardworking genius. He arrived in Canada at the age of twenty-five from Delhi when his wife got her PR.

In Delhi, he used to work at an IT firm. When he arrived here, he decided to start afresh as he didn't really like working as an 'IT guy'. The first few months, he started working as a door to door salesman selling expensive toiletry products on a monthly subscription basis in upmarket neighborhoods.

He has learnt that instead of simply repeating what the sales script told him to say to customers, it worked better if he simply stood on their doorstep with the product in his hand

and a smile, because the product was beautifully packaged with various soaps, creams, talcs, bath salts wrapped in a gift basket.

People, especially women, excitedly opened their door thinking that someone had sent them a present. When Brijesh introduced himself and his product, they lapped it up.

He ended up selling them a year's subscription.

Speaking to customers at their doorstep eliminated his inhibitions and polished his negotiation skills. He was the top salesman of the company that year.

During night time, he started studying for the insurance exams to get an insurance selling license. He cleared his exams with flying colours and got a job offer from a huge insurance conglomerate where he started working.

According to him, he had thoroughly understood the Canadian insurance system early on.

It was only a matter of which area he should focus on in that field. The insurance industry hasn't changed much in the past century, except a few things becoming more organized and automated, but largely it is still archaic. By the age of twenty-nine, he had a company house, a car, two assistants and ten juniors working under him. People who had been working for over ten years in the company hadn't been able to achieve this.

One thing he noticed while working at the company was that the housing claims suddenly went up during winter time. In Canada, water pipes would often burst during winters because the water inside them would expand as it got close to freezing, increasing the pressure inside the pipe.

This would cause the basements of houses to become flooded. This in turn, led the owners to file for compensation from their respective insurance companies.

He smelled opportunity.

In the insurance sector, housing claims were still somewhat an untapped field which led him to start to work on his dream of starting his own company.

Also, by that time, he also started receiving independent consulting offers. So, lack of stability wouldn't be an issue as he could now work on his own time consulting and earn more than his salaried job.

Anton had arrived in Canada in the 1980s. He was from a very poor family from Kazakhstan and his parents worked as labourers in various construction firms. From a very young age, Anton was quieter than other kids. While the other kids would be out playing most of the time, he would sit for hours and observe various people in his village marketplace. Most of the vendors and merchants knew him by name and would call him for small odd jobs, involving mostly labour-oriented work.

One day, a fruit vendor named Nurik asked Anton to look after his shop for a few hours as he had to attend some personal matter. Anton was only fourteen at the time. By the time he returned, Anton had sold almost half his inventory, leaving him flabbergasted.

When asked as to how he managed to sell such a huge lot, Anton replied that he simply posted a small handwritten sign saying '70% discount'. He had marked up the price of his least selling fruit by about three times. So, the fruit which was priced at sixty kazakh tenge was marked up to two hundred and then sold at sixty, 'after special discount'.

When a customer enquired, he said that his boss has a special offer for only five customers per day if they buy at least two kilos. Customers bought four.

Within an hour, word had spread among the walk-ins' and people started pouring in.

Anton replicated that offer to include more varieties of fruit from the vendor's inventory. He played with the psychology of customers who felt privileged to have availed such an offer as it made them feel special. Nurik was mighty impressed.

He offered Anton two hundred kazakh tenge a month to work with him after his school. Anton said that instead of a salary, he wanted a share of the profits. Nurik gave him a smack on the head and told him to go home. Anton walked home slowly, with tears in his eyes, cursing Nurik. He felt that the fruit vendor was short-sighted and dumb.

A week later, Nurik came by his house and told him that he could offer him a 10 % share of the profits.

Anton negotiated share to 20 %. Nurik had no option but to accept.

For the first time in his life, Anton felt important. A person, at least thirty years older was in a business partnership with him. He worked with Nurik for about a year before his parents decided to migrate to Canada. During his first year in Canada, Anton underwent depression as he missed his home and his country. He was used to living alone, but in Canada, he felt lonelier as he didn't know the language and it didn't help that his parents were working most of the time. He decided that the first thing he would do was to learn English. He joined an English speaking class from his savings from Kazakhstan which amounted to almost nothing when converted into dollars.

Even though he struggled initially, Anton soon was speaking the language fluently, and within six months, he got a job as a telesales executive selling window frames to customers. His knack for sales was his strong suit and soon enough, he too was amongst the top salesmen of his company, at a tender age of seventeen.

By the time he was nineteen, he stole the customer database from that company to start his own small business of selling window frames. Within five years, he had expanded his business to three cities in Ontario, employing forty people, and was a self-made millionaire. He bought a rundown strip club outside of Toronto, had it refurbished and ventured into the night club business. He liked quite a few materialistic pleasures such as cars (he drove a Range Rover and an Audi), had a large multi-storied mansion outside Toronto and loved to go on holidays to the Bahamas.

His company graduated from selling window frames to offering services such as home renovations to his customers. It was during this time he met Brijesh.

Brijesh and Anton hit it off from the word go. They had similar entrepreneurial passions and Brijesh learned a great deal from Anton, who although younger than him, possessed a great deal of experience.

They decided to start a company together called Inventory Storage Solutions (ISS) with Anton investing a million dollars in the same. Within the first four months, their company was profitable. Using Brijesh's contacts within the insurance industry, they were able to get work from the first day itself. The insurance companies preferred to work on the large claims themselves and found it cumbersome and expensive to deal with small claims. These small housing claims, which mostly consisted of flooded basements, were outsourced to ISS. Brijesh had spotted the right opportunity at the right time.

For ISS, Brijesh rented a large storage warehouse in Toronto to store the household items, furniture etc., which were recovered from the damaged houses.

Items collected from the houses were bubble wrapped and then segregated into salvageable, non-salvageable and scrap.

Salvageable stood for those items which could be repaired and restored. Non-salvageable stood for those items for which claims were issued after deducting depreciation. And finally, scrap, well was scrap.

ISS charged the insurance companies an hourly rate depending on the services offered, whether it was site inspection, segregation of inventory, storage or claim verification.

One thing which ISS benefitted from was that it didn't have any permanent staff on their payroll. All the labour staff was from Anton's company and shuffled between both the companies depending on the work load. This was a huge bonus as the liability of ISS was reduced; as it could now have a lot of workers on call without having to keep them on a permanent basis. Although training was provided to them for their additional work duties at ISS.

Brijesh and I used to meet quite often during the initial startup days of ISS. He had a Greek driver named Tomas who used to drive him around the city and he also utilized him as a labour worker during his 'non-driving' hours, paying him extra for that time.

Tomas is literally a multi-tasker as he is Brijesh's personal assistant arranging his schedules, driver and worker. Every evening, Brijesh would pick me up and we would go have a few beers and discuss things. Brijesh drives around in a Honda Civic and unlike Anton does not care for materialistic pleasures. He has a very simple dressing sense, doesn't care about how he looks and isn't a big spender. His only two pleasures are smoking and drinking; his favourite Guinness beer. But he is very focused about his work ethic and his relations with his colleagues and staff.

He used to empower me with his wisdom, things he has learnt on a daily basis on running an organization and stories about Anton. While I have only once met Anton, one thing which strikes me is he is like a combination of a dolphin and a shark who is your best friend and guide if you do your work properly, but would bite your head off if you don't – charming, yet lethal.

Brijesh tells me that he sees a lot of potential in me and invites me to work with him handling the inventory management side of things and getting the process more streamlined and organized at ISS.

I would accompany the staff at the house site for which the owners had filed for a claim. While the workers would wrap and package the household items, I instill a system wherein at the site itself the goods could be categorized instead of back at the warehouse. This saves ISS a lot of money as they could utilize their staff for other duties since the goods arrive at the warehouse, properly segregated.

One evening, Anton invites me and Brijesh to his strip club on a weekend. I find strip clubs a bit depressing, but needless to say, I am more excited on having a one-on-one with Anton.

Tomas calls me to inform that Brijesh will be meeting me outside Dundas metro station at 7 p.m. from where they will pick me up to go to Anton's club. I manage to reach the metro station around fifteen past seven as the trains are very crowded in the evening and I have to miss two trains before I get on the third one.

Tomas is waiting for me outside the station who asks me to hurry as we are running late. As I enter the car, Brijesh is already 'happy high' and hands me a can of his favourite beer. Since the strip club is located outside of Toronto, he says we rather start with our pre-drinks on the journey itself.

I say sure why the hell not!

On our way to the club, it starts raining. A bout of unseasonal rains does occur once in a while in Toronto. Brijesh takes out his phone and dials Anton's number to ask about his whereabouts and also to inform him that we might be a bit late because of the traffic caused by the rains.

Anton picks up after two rings and sounds inebriated. There are sounds of giggling in the background.

Putting the phone on speaker,

Brijesh: "Anton sir, how arrrrr you! It is raining like a bitch here!"

Anton (speaking in a higher pitch): "Mr B, come my friend, come fast. I have a present for you. I'm sure you can hear it in the background!"

Brijesh: "Hahaa, you are very kind, but I am a married man. Give my present my best regards."

Anton: "You Indians! You have my respect! I will give her your regards all night but first get here so that we can drink our hearts out, NOSTROVIA!!"

Brijesh: "Nostrovia *mere dost*, we will be there as soon as possible!"

Brijesh cuts the call and turns towards me.

Me: "Hahaha! That was funny Brijesh. How often do you get these 'presents'?"

Brijesh (looking a bit worried): "Tomas, turn the car around; we won't be going to meet Anton. Take me to the pub on Yonge."

Me: "Oye, everything ok? You sound a bit tensed."

Brijesh: "It's a good thing it started raining. We won't be meeting Anton tonight because judging by his voice, he is doing the combination today. And whenever that happens, it sure turns out to be an awful night."

Me: "Combination?"

Brijesh: "It's one of those days when Anton starts the night by snorting cocaine. After a round of coke, he does a few shots of alcohol followed by more coke. Usually when we are out, Anton rarely does any drugs and only drinks vodka, but if he is angry or depressed about something, he does the combination. And the night usually ends up in a bad mess. Last time, cops had arrived due to the ruckus Anton had created. He had thrown his boot at one of the bouncers at a pub because the bouncer was staring at him in a funny way."

Me: "Wow! Who would have known Anton had this mad side to him. Do you think we can go meet him today? I am kind of curious to see him now that you've mentioned."

Brijesh: "No Gaurav, trust me, with him, you never know which way the night might proceed. It's better we go to some pub on our own."

Me: "Come on man, let's meet him for an hour at least. Then I'll tell him that I have to leave due to some excuse which I will make up"

Brijesh: "*Thik hai,* but don't tell me that I didn't warn you. Sorry about that Tomas, please turn the car around. We are going to meet Anton."

Tomas looks visibly annoyed and looks at me in the rear view mirror. I smile back.

Thirty minutes later, we pull up outside the strip joint. It looks fairly crowded. I see a lot of bikers with big tummies and beards. Looks like one of those biker joints they show in Hollywood movies.

Snaking our way through the crowd, we enter the place. It is dimly lit apart from the stage. The girl who is currently on stage, dancing provocatively and stripping, is getting a lot of whistles and cheers from the crowd.

Off topic, but there is also an all you can eat buffet for $30. We see Anton sitting in the VIP section which has four large couches and a low centre table in between. Anton is crouched over the table with his head very close to the tabletop as if trying to find something. As we walk towards him, I realize that he is not trying to find something, but is doing what appears snorting lines of cocaine. He has two girls sitting with him who also partake. His face lights up on seeing Brijesh and me.

Anton: "Glad you could make it guys! Welcome, welcome to my humble abode. This is Tasha and Tammy. Girls, say hi to our guests."

Both Tasha and Tammy give us a flying kiss. Brijesh and I smile back at them and sit on the sofas. Anton snaps his fingers and magically a waitress appears carrying a sparkler and a bucket with Grey Goose vodkas. She pours the vodka in shot glasses for all of us. And we drink.

Before we know it, we have finished about two bottles of vodka.

Both me and Brijesh are pretty much knackered at this point.

Anton is on another planet.

He is making out with one girl after another. From that point on, an incident followed which I remember literally in slow motion.

Something flies through the air and hits Anton's head. It hits my head too, and Brijesh's chest. Before I can realize what is going on, more unidentified flying objects are being hurled at us. As an instinct, I duck to crawl out of the target zone where these objects are being thrown, but due to my drunkenness, the moment I duck, I am flat on the floor. Lying flat on my stomach and my face touching the floor provide me one important intel. Close to the floor, I try to focus my eyes and clear my vision to see the 'object' lying next to me which was being thrown at us.

It is a champagne glass.

Thousands of shards of it on the floor. I am behind enemy lines and have to get out of the kill zone. I start crawling – one feet, two feet.

Soon, I am ten feet away and out of harm's way.

Same cannot be said for Brijesh and Anton. While Brijesh is protecting himself with a cushion from the sofa, albeit unsuccessfully, Anton has simply passed out.

Finally, I manage to stand up with some help from the bouncers of the club. Sensing my bewilderment, the bouncer smiles and points towards the source of this barrage. It is a bunch of women throwing champagne glasses out of the bar at Anton.

Bouncer man (pointing towards one of the women): "That is Anton sir's wife."

Me: "What the… how the… WHAAAT! What the hell! I didn't know he was married!"

Bouncer man (thoroughly enjoying the show): "Yes, he is married alright. His wife got her girlfriends along to teach him a lesson. Although seeing that sir's passed out, I don't think it is of much use tonight. Alright ladies, let's break it up. Ma'am, please put that glass down. I think sir has been knocked out."

Anton's wife (her face filled with rage and eyes full of tears): "Lying piece of shit! Fucking hate you Antiii!! You said you were in Ottawa for a business meeting!! I will make you fucking sell this place!!"

Bouncer man: "Ma'am please, let's all calm down here. Please let me escort you to your car."

Anton's wife (not hearing what he said, starting running towards Anton with her fist clenched): "Fuckkkkkking assssshole!"

The bouncers catch up to her just in time as she is about to hit Anton in the groin. Ouch!

Kicking and screaming, the bouncer gently lifts her and takes her to her car. Her friends follow her before hurling curses at a passed out Anton.

I look at Brijesh. He is sitting upright on the sofa now, with a dazed look in his eyes and a few cuts on his head. A minute later, he passes out also.

Anton is soon ushered into his car and a bouncer goes along with his driver to drop him home. Tomas soon shows up and both of us carry Brijesh back to the car. Tomas stops by a hospital to tend to our cuts and bruises and then drops Brijesh home first, before dropping me.

I reach home and sit on my bed for what seems like a long time, thinking about the events that have unfolded tonight. It is like a scene from a mafia movie has just played in front of me.

Brijesh calls me the next morning to apologize about last night. He tells me that despite knowing and working with Anton for over two years, even he didn't know that Anton has a wife as he has never made him meet her, or even mentioned her, as a matter of fact.

One surprising thing is that Anton comes to visit one day, a month after the incident, at one of the houses which we are surveying for an insurance claim. He simply hangs around the site for an hour. Before leaving, he tells me something very bizarre. He tells me that I am doing a very good job, but he foresees me quitting ISS and starting my own business.

I do that soon enough.

After working at ISS for a few more months, I quit before returning to India to pursue my entrepreneurial venture.

P.S.: Anton sold his strip club and turned a new leaf after that night's incident, more or less. Rumour has it that his wife threatened to divorce him and take half his fortune which apparently knocked some sense into him.

Lift Off

Tring Tring. Tring Tring. Tring tring

"Hello?"

"Mr Guravvey?"

"Gaurav?"

"Err… Mr G..A..U..R..A..V?"

"Yes, correct. It's pronounced as Gaurav."

"Hi, Gooorav. This is Sandra calling from Centennial College, Student Induction Committee. I am calling to inform you that we will be hosting an induction and introduction to Canada session on the fourth of January. We look forward to having all the Strategic Management's students there."

"Sure Sandra. Thanks, I'll see you then."

"You're welcome Gooorav. Please reach by 12 p.m. at the Progress Campus."

(Why the fuck can't anyone pronounce my name correctly in this bloody country!)

"Will do Sandra."

Click

Hi.

My name as you've just read above is Gaurav.

There are high chances you should be able to pronounce my name. Since, I'm assuming you, kind reader, are Indian.

If you're not, well then here's how you pronounce my name.

Gau... as in how you say 'go in god.' Rav as in shove but with an R.

Get it?

Maybe not. I'm equally bad at explaining pronunciations as you've probably guessed by now.

(God and shove? Haha, yup I'm awful at this.)

Anyway, so that point being, folks of foreign origin for some reason find it hard to pronounce it.

Guravveyy, Goro, Gura, Garav are a few of their attempts to pronounce it.

Not even close.

Sitting on my bed, in my matchbox sized room, I reminisce on the past few weeks before my arrival in Toronto.

One fine day not that far away...

Me: "Papa?"

Papa: "Hmm?"

Me: "Papa, I want to go to Canada for my further studies."

Papa: "Canada? Are you sure you want to go there?"

Me: "Ya, papa. Out of all the places I've researched, this is the best option. Will ask around about it."

Papa: "Hmm, actually, your cousin Richa is also working there, in Toronto right? Why don't you speak to your *fufaji* today, he'll give you a better insight."

Me: "Ya, I had a word with Richa last week. Canada will give me great international exposure and the cost of the programme is not exorbitant compared to other places."

Papa: "But do you want to move there? Research properly and then decide. I'm fine as long as you are happy."

Well, that's my dad for you. Always supportive of whatever I do.

Love you Papa.

My conversation with fufaji lasts for nearly an hour, wherein he briefs me about Canada, the pros and cons of living there once you are a resident.

A few pros include free health care, strong economy, and quality life and immigrant friendliness.

Cons included weather, weather and weather. And a penchant for being cut off from the rest of the world.

Canadian winters are quite harsh and can last as long as seven to eight months, even more in certain places. I did my research and decided to pursue a programme called Strategic Management Post Grad. Basically, it is like MBA on steroids. Very intense and covers all management subjects, plus the practical stuff. The programme is offered by Centennial College, which is a community college in Scarborough.

Well, after tenth grade, my grades literally went on a downswing. I was an ace student during my school days, but as soon as I got out of school, my mind wandered. During my junior college, i.e. eleventh and twelfth grade, I scraped through with about 60% marks. I then went on to pursue engineering which is the safest degree you can get in India. After speaking to everyone in my family and extended family, it was suggested that since I was a Science stream student, engineering was an extension.

By safest I mean, if you are pursuing engineering, you are considered extremely wise for making a safe choice which safeguards your future.

Arre, degree hain na, isiliye!

Neighbours/relatives/'*log*' also are not too rattled since you are doing 'something with your life'. You also have an added benefit of being safely within the Indian society's education

system which segregates people majorly into two categories:-
Engineering, Medical and CA (Charted Accountant).

Erm, I mean three categories.

I have studied engineering in Pune in a college called
Vishwakarma Institute of Technology. Studying in Pune has
taught me the importance of independence and also added a
little sense of responsibility.

Living at home, one tends to take for granted the little
things which magically happen every day. Like how your
clothes magically appear inside your cupboard, cleaned and
ironed. Or that food is cooked every day, fresh and served hot
for you. Milk inside your fridge always gets replenished and
so does the water. Who is this strange and powerful magician?
Your mom, obviously, or your dad.

Or any other parental figure who protects you and looks
after you.

On one side, we are happy that we are moving away from
our home and finally tasting 'freedom'. But after a month or
so, on the other side, after seeing our rented room in a mess,
fed up of eating outside food, groggily waking up every day
early morning to take milk from the *doodhwala*, selfishly, we
begin missing home. Living in the hostel first and then in a
flat with room-mates, we learn how to balance studies, fun,
housework all together. Some of my best friends are from my
engineering days.

And engineering isn't a piece of cake either. Our teachers
make sure that we suffer under useless rote learning, which
on most occasions is hardly practical or applicable in real life.
But most importantly, we learn how to manage stress. A stress
management module is a free inclusion of every engineering
programme. It is during this time that we really use cuss words

to the fullest, for they serve as an important tool to relieve us of our stress. (albeit temporarily.)

So, after the roller-coaster that is engineering, I pass out in a year that was hit by heavy recession.

Job scarcity then was at its peak as hardly any companies came on campus to recruit that year. I came back to Mumbai and joined a small IT/BPO type company in Kandivali. The company specialized in online tendering and would put up tenders of various companies on its website and those interested could access those tenders for a fee.

I lasted there for exactly four days.

The whole company had their office on two floors inside a small shopping complex and 'working there' depressed the fuck out of me. The company, the employees, everything – I hated it. I literally ran during a lunch break as I could not see myself working there.

Again, I was at a crossroads in life when everyone started asking what I intended to do now that my engineering was over.

That's when Canada came into the picture.

After the formalities were done, admission to that college confirmed, my programme was scheduled to begin on the third of January. I booked my flight tickets for the twenty-second of December. I wanted to experience a white Christmas amidst the snow in Toronto and also bring in the New Year there before my studies started.

Centennial College has several campuses and one of them is located in Scarborough which is a suburb of Toronto, located on the eastern side of the city.

I booked the cheapest flight; total duration of the journey was about nineteen hours with a stopover at Amsterdam. Needless to say, I was pretty psyched about the whole thing.

Finally, D-day arrived. My parents were excited yet sad to see me go for such a long time.

At least when I was in Pune, I could come back every month, but now I was really going *'saat samundar paar'*.

Such frequent trips are not possible. My mom gets a little teary-eyed when she bids me goodbye. My sister who is a huge foodie like me kept suggesting the things I should eat in Canada. Especially desserts, as my sister literally has dreams of desserts. No, I'm not kidding.

Dad tells me to make him proud. It is an emotional moment for everyone. I take everyone's blessings and leave for the airport.

My flight is around midnight, and I tell everyone that I prefer to go to the airport alone. Check in done, formalities complete, I wait to board at my boarding gate.

There is only one small issue. I am two hours early. Yep, in the Indian tradition of reaching the airport early so as to not 'miss your flight', I reach pretty early.

I use the internet for a bit, but get bored as all I can see on my Facebook wall is people wishing me a happy journey and best wishes for Canada.

I see a message from my cousin who lives there also telling me to carry warm clothes as it is freaking freezing there.

I decide to take a nap for a bit as there is nothing to do now but wait for the boarding to start. After informing the airline ground staff to wake me up when the boarding starts, I slept.

After what seems like an eternity, I am woken up by a tall smiling guy informing me that I should board the plane. The flight is packed like sardines in a can. My seat is located right at the end of the plane. I have to literally squish through the people standing in the aisle putting their luggage in the overhead compartments. Indians are the noisiest lot, making a lot of commotion for no god damn reason.

On reaching my seat, I see that there is a young guy sitting next to me, playing games on his phone. We greet each other as I sit down. He tells me that his name is Daniel. He's playing 'Need for Speed' on his phone and I tell him that it is one of my favourite games ever. I am a game boy myself and love gaming in general. My favourite genres are racing, strategy and fps (first person shooter).

We hit it off immediately for our love for games and end up discussing a lot of the current games out in the market in depth. Soon, our flight takes off and we are cruising at about thirty thousand feet and sipping chilled beer. Our conversation veers from games towards movies. He is a really avid movie buff also.

He really loves to talk and hails from a small town called Harrison in Montana.

The population of his hometown, he tells me, in less than two hundred people.

Less than two hundred? That is like the population of a crowded Mumbai pub on a weekend.

He is studying mechanical engineering and had come to Pune, India for an internship. Now that his internship is complete, he is on his way home.

We order for three more beers. Each.

Me: "So, I'm sure everyone has asked you this clichéd question about how was your 'Indian' experience. What I want to ask you is, would you want to stay back if given the opportunity?"

Daniel: "Haha, yes, yes, that is one common question I get asked more often than not. And my answer is that it has been a mixed bag. On one side, I have really learned from the ground up everything there is to know about the technical and realistic side of manufacturing of parts. I would be on the job floor for fifteen hours straight with the employees there, working and learning at the same time. That part I loved because each employee there was so helpful and would be patient with me, which really boosted my confidence. Indians are the best in the world, in my opinion, when it comes to people and relationships. On the other hand, I absolutely despised a few things like hygiene which I feel Indians need a huge lesson on. I mean, people openly shitting everywhere is not a good sign!"

Me: "Hahahhaha, yes, so you've seen the shitting on the railway tracks, I'm guessing. Yes, we as a society do not put basic hygiene as our priority. We keep our homes clean, but dirty our surroundings thinking the government has the duty to keep our roads clean. It's a fucked up archaic mindset."

Daniel: "I know Goorav. This one time, I saw a guy talking on his phone while shitting. I mean, he was literally squatting down on the road and talking, loud as fuck, while doing his business. I and another friend of mine were in splits!"

Me: "Hahahahahaha! That's hilarious! But you know, the area which I live in Bombay has a shoreline. And along the shoreline, there is also a huge area occupied by slums. So, every morning, a lot of these guys make their way to the beach, just where the waves end and well, they do their business."

Daniel: "WHAT!"

Me: "Hahahahahahahahahahahahahaa!"

Daniel: "Goorav, I think I just lost my appetite."

I call for another round of beers. The air hostess is now visibly annoyed by our incessant laughing and lets us know that this is the last beer that we will be getting as they have run out.

Daniel comes up with an easy solution to this dilemma. He tells her that we will switch to drinking whiskey from here on.

By the time the flight lands in Schiphol airport, Amsterdam, we are fast asleep (passed out).

We are rudely woken up by the same airhostess who curtly tells us to get the fuck off the plane, but in a nicer way, obviously.

Her exact words are: "Sir, I request you to deboard the plane now. You are delaying the staff from leaving."

Ok then.

We groggily get off the plane and sit down at the nearest waiting couches at the airport. Daniel goes to check if his flight is on time while I attempt to connect to the airport Wi-Fi on my phone to inform my folks back home that I have reached Amsterdam. Soon, I am online and send a Whats app to my parents.

Both my parents are quite tech savvy and enjoy using WhatsApp and Facebook. Although sometimes, this can be a double-edged sword. For most teenagers/young adults, one of the most dreaded things is getting a friend request on Facebook from your parents. With me it happened as well, but in a bit of a funny yet scary way.

Living on my own in another city whilst completing my engineering studies changed me drastically as a person. For the better. Hence, to commemorate the changes, challenges, joys and sorrows which I have faced as a person, I decide to get a tattoo to immortalize those moments. After a lot of contemplation, speaking to friends, doing research online, I make up my mind and decide that my first tattoo would be that of a phoenix. Phoenix being the mythological bird that rises from the ashes every time it dies to live another life, rejuvenated. To me it is the ultimate symbol of perpetual continuance and change which is the essence of life. An important thing engineering taught me is that in life, one should not be bogged down by failures and sorrows. These are a part and parcel of life and only those who can welcome change learn from it; those who are ready to adapt are the ones who succeed. Not the ones who are stubborn, crib and do nothing.

Anyway, so, I go to a tattoo parlour in Koregaon Park in Pune with three of my friends to finally get a tattoo. I decide to get it in the area between my upper back and neck and literally on my spinal cord. Not the best of places when getting a first tattoo. Not only does it hurt like hell, to the amusement of my friends who are busy shooting videos of my misery, it takes about three hours to complete. So, the first thing which I do after getting a tattoo is to click a picture and change my profile picture on Facebook. All of us go to get a few drinks to celebrate my tattoo and I forget about the picture.

The next morning, I see about thirty likes on my picture, two messages and two friend requests.

The first message read 'Hi beta, nice tattoo. When did you get it? I have sent you a friend request.'

The second message is rather short. It says 'Is your tattoo permanent?'

And both the friend requests as you've guessed by now are from my parents.

Shit.

Fearing the worst, I decide to call them and break the news. Unlike what I perceived online, my parents are very cool about it and pleasantly surprised.

Anyway, so back in Schiphol.

After informing my parents, I fall asleep again. David comes and wakes me up saying that his flight is on time and that he must leave now as the boarding gate is in another part of the airport, which is quite far from where we are currently. We bid each other goodbye and before leaving, he tells me that he might stay on in India as his boss has invited him for a full time job. I congratulate him and he wishes me the best of luck for my trip forward.

I decide to drink some water and head to the washroom to wash my face and to brush my teeth. Feeling refreshed, I decide to check on my connecting flight status from Amsterdam to Toronto. There is a giant television screen right outside the bathroom as I emerge.

I scan the screen to try to locate my flight number from the hundreds that are scheduled. For some reason, I cannot find it. I stand there, searching for about fifteen minutes but still I cannot locate my flight details. My flight leaves in about three-and-a-half hours and exasperated, I decide to go to the airline counter to enquire.

When I reach the counter, there is a lot of commotion and a huge queue. Soon, there is an announcement from the ground staff that our flight has run into some operational trouble and is delayed by sixteen hours. By now everyone is screaming and cursing the airline for the delay.

I, on the other hand, am ecstatic.

I feel happy that I can now go outside and explore Amsterdam as I have a lot of time on my hand. When suddenly, I hear a pop go off in my head.

Which is the sound of my bubble bursting. I realize that I need a Schengen visa to go outside.

My wonderful Indian passport requires us to have a visa to visit any and every country. Well, almost.

Dejected, I feel a bit like Tom Hanks from the movie *Terminal* who was stuck at the airport because his country no longer existed.

The airline to 'compensate' us for the delay, handed us twenty Euros worth of food and drink coupons.

Hence with nothing to do now but wait, I decided to make lemonade out of lemons. Explore the giant Schiphol airport of Amsterdam.

I grab a tuna baguette (my favourite) from a small bakery paying with my coupon and head out to explore. Since this is the first time I have ventured out of Asia, I can't help but admire the amazing dressing sense of people even during winter time. Perfectly fitted and trendy coats, overcoats, hats, scarves, boots make us Asians look underdressed.

Indians by any standard are not the best dressed anyway during winters, in my opinion, but here I feel folks do take their looks quite seriously. Only during the wedding season, a majority of us take the effort to look sharp whether we are attending one or getting hitched.

After aimlessly roaming around the airport for about an hour, I am thoroughly bored and now cursing the stupid airline. I decide to find a chair where I can sit down or sleep.

Yup, I love sleeping and I can sleep anywhere, anytime on cue. I've had some of the soundest naps while traveling via buses, cars, trains or planes. There is a humming sound in the background either from the engine noise or the turning wheels which strangely, I find soothing.

On my search to find a good seat, I encounter a casino.

Yes, you read that right – a casino, in the middle of the airport.

I feel that while building the airport, there must have been a lot of discussions and brainstorming as to how to make sure the people are happy, comfortable and satisfied when they enter Amsterdam.

One guy would have said, 'Let's make a robust and accessible transport system within the airport so that people can easily commute from one part of the airport to the other.' Another would have said, 'Let's make sure we have plenty of rest rooms and lounge chairs for people to relax on as well as free Wi-Fi for our guests to use.'

After hearing all the ideas, the boss would be like, 'That's great. Let's us proceed with those.'

When suddenly a guy from the back would say, 'How 'bout we add a casino? Nothing makes people happier than a casino. Yes, sure they might get poorer after losing money, but poor people are the happiest, right?'

And BAM! There you go – a casino, for your happiness, comfort and satisfaction. I enter the casino after they check my passport to make sure I am not underage. The place is not very big, but it's not small either.

There are three large tables hosting blackjack and roulette. And about twenty slot machines. After lurking around watching people gamble on the tables, I decide that since I have hardly any money, I'll play on the slot machine for one Euro which was equivalent to about sixty rupees at that time. Today, it's around seventy.

I put a euro in the slot machine which gobbles it up and I start playing. There are about a hundred different combinations due to which I keep winning or losing fraction amounts. My single coin deposit lasts for about three hours. And by the time I get up, I have won fifty cents.

Going to the casino wasn't entirely a bad idea, after all, as not only have I passed time, but also won. The feeling of winning is fun even though it is only fifty cents, for a while.

The remaining hours pass by sleeping, eating and having an occasional beer. I make sure I fully utilize my free food and drink coupons.

Finally, boarding begins. I am not really looking forward to flying as it has been a really long layover. I enter the flight and navigate to my seat. This flight will reach Toronto in about nine hours and being a last minute replacement, ours is a smaller plane with no 'in-flight entertainment', not even music. Basically, nothing to do for nine hours but bang your head against the window. By now I am quite cranky and tired and seeing the two empty seats next to me in my row, I take up the whole space and stretch my legs. Soon, I doze off. A short while later, I feel a tap on my shoulder.

A rather large African American woman wearing a rather large straw hat is waving her hands and asking me to move. I have dozed off on the entire row of seats and my feet were on her aisle seat. Needless to say, she was annoyed.

Not being able to take my eyes off her straw hat, I apologize and quickly return to my normal sitting position. She sits on her seat grumbling and fastens her belt, placing her hat on her lap. Everyone around us is casually sneaking a peek at her hat which is ginormous.

Distracting myself from the 'curious case of the straw hat', I look outside the window to see that it is snowing quite heavily and there are these large crane like machines spraying some liquid on the wings of the plane. I assume it's to prevent the flaps, engine manifolds from freezing.

I pray that there aren't any more delays and that we reach Toronto ASAP.

Another person joins us in our row occupying the middle seat. For my travel weary sore eyes, her presence for some reason instantly brightens my mood.

She is wearing a bright pink top and jeans with her hair neatly tied in a pony. Her perfume is quite strong with a fruity smell to it. And yes, she is ravishing to look at.

It is not every day that a stunning looking girl comes and sits next to you during a journey. Every guy, whenever traveling alone via any public mode of transport secretly hopes that a beautiful stranger comes and sits next to him, sharing his journey.

I too unconsciously start to fix my hair, but I know that I look a mess. After traveling for over a day without having a bath, I know I am not looking my best or smelling great either.

The large grumpy woman is also somewhat happy to have her sitting with us. She smiles and gets up from her seat, to allow her to sit.

Well, this last leg of our journey won't be so bad after all.

Soon the flight takes off smoothly and the airhostesses appear with refreshments. The large grumpy woman has transformed into a large 'smiley' woman and is the first to introduce herself to both of us.

Big Woman: "I hate theys flying biness, why can't em folks just travel by road. Makes me so cranky and nauseous. I'm Claire, by the way, darlings."

Hot Girl: "Hi Claire! I'm Jessica. This stupid airline made me so mad. This has been the longest layover for me. I'm never flying with this fucking airline again!"

Me: "Well, I've been traveling for the past two days and I've still not reached Toronto. I'm Gaurav from the land of Bollywood."

I don't know why I said the latter part. It was cheesy as hell. But since it led to both of them guffawing, I guess 'cheese' sometimes works.

Claire: "Guraa! Hahahahaha, you from Mumbai? I like Sharook Khaa, Kapoo! I've seen *Pardis* and *Kooch Kooch Hota Haai!*"

Me: 'Oh, *Pardes* and *Kuch Kuch Hota Hai* you mean. Yup, I've seen them; his name is Shah Rukh Khan. Kapoor is another actor called Shahid Kapoor.'

Claire: 'Yes, yes, oh Sharook, damn he so handsome. So, he must be like a huge movie star in India!'

Jessica: 'Hey Claire, I've seen *Pardis* also. I was living in India for about three years, in Delhi and Pune.'

Me: 'Oh! Well, I've lived for about four years in Pune. I have studied engineering there.'

Jessica: 'I like Pune more than Delhi; people in Delhi stare a lot. And I'm like one-quarter Indian so, I understand a bit of Hindi.'

Me: 'Yup, that's Delhi for you. As a person from Mumbai, I have mixed views about Delhi. The food, a few of the people I know from that city are fantastic. But a lot of whom I've encountered are way too racist, chauvinist and narrow-minded.'

Claire: 'Sounds a lot like 'em folks from Winnipeg!'
Me: 'Winnipeg?'

Jessica: 'Yes, Gaurav, there have been a lot of cases of abuse and racial discrimination there. Really awful stuff.'

Me: 'Hey, you pronounced my name correctly!'

Jessica: 'Well, I had a friend from Delhi called Gaurav also.'

Me: 'Oh! Ok.'

Claire: 'I also said your name correctly! Guraave!'

Me: 'Hahaha, sure you did, Claire. Not!'

Claire goes off to sleep while I and Jessica continue talking. I am by now totally smitten by her and her perfume. She goes on to tell me about the friends she has made in India and the experiences she had. Turns out that she lives very close to where my college is in Toronto, in an area called Scarborough.

Me: 'Umm, Jessica? Would you like to go out for a coffee or something over this weekend?'

Jessica: 'Aww… Gaurav, that's sweet, I have a boyfriend. Sorry! If you want, you can Facebook me!'

Me (pop goes my bubble): 'Uh, yea, sure.'

There is nothing worse in the world than to be 'friend zoned'. That too on Facebook!

Jessica (trying to cheer me up): 'Christmas is an amazing time to be in Toronto, city is really lit up and soon Boxing Day will be coming!'

Me: 'Oh, what's Boxing Day?'

Jessica: 'Only the biggest sale in Canada!! People wait for this day all year long to shop because things are available on massive discounts! Last year, my boyfriend got his Xbox at 60 % discount! You should definitely check it out.'

Me: 'Oh sweet. I don't think I'll buy anything this year but I would love to check it out.'

I decide to order a beer and sleep it off for the rest of the journey otherwise I would be very tired by the time we reach Toronto.

Pretty soon, I nod off to sleep, induced due to my travel weariness. I wake up with a jolt when the pilot makes an announcement that we will soon be landing in Toronto. I thought I have slept only for about fifteen minutes but actually I was out for about four hours.

Soon, the plane starts its descent and we enter the Toronto airspace.

Touching down smoothly, the plane taxies on the runway before coming to a complete halt at its designated parking spot.

Passengers start to deboard the plane when Jessica turns towards me and gives me a big hug, wishing me good luck for my studies. Claire too wishes me a Merry Christmas before deboarding herself.

Stepping down from the plane into the jet bridge, my spirits rise and finally I feel a bit of relief.

Toronto, I have arrived!

O Canada, The True North, strong and free!

Here I come to meet thee!

P.S.: A few months down the line, as fate would have it, it is Jessica who helps me find a house on rent after I move out from Mr Bhavesh Shah's house.

Rabbit hole

*M*y programme at Centennial College attracts students from literally all over the globe. Nigeria, Ghana, Iran, Russia, Slovakia, Pakistan, Bangladesh, Canada and India, of course. Indians constitute for about 20% of the total class population while the next highest are Russians and Nigerians.

The issue is that I cannot relate to the Indians in my programme at all.

Or to a lot of Indians I have met in Toronto in general. Coming from a city like Mumbai, I thought Indians living abroad would have a broader perspective of life and would be more progressive.

The truth on the other hand is completely opposite.

People in cities like Mumbai, Bangalore, Pune, Calcutta, Gangtok, Shillong and a lot of other Indian cities have evolved by leaps and bounds during the last twenty or so years, their mindsets changed. Even though politicos are trying hard to keep our mindset backward, with a majority part of India being in a state of flux, I personally believe we are slowly evolving.

Here, in Canada however, is a slightly different story.

I feel that a lot of NRIs who arrived here thirty/forty years ago are stuck in that time capsule. Their thoughts echo with what the earlier Indian mindsets were. Also, a huge part of the new age immigrants come from small villages and towns of Punjab and Gujarat; they take huge loans, sell their ancestral land in search of utopia in a foreign land. They too suffer from this apathy.

I get a reverse culture shock after meeting my Indian classmates and a lot of other NRIs. I am appalled by their pre-historic mindset, especially men, who was extremely chauvinist and racist.

They are equally perplexed by me too.

I usually hang out with three girls from my class, a Nigerian named Diana, an Indian from Dubai named Divya and a Bangladeshi named Amina.

Diana used to work for FedEx in her country before her boss recommended that she should study abroad because she had a lot of potential. He also told her that after she had completed her management programme, he would recommend her to the FedEx office in Toronto.

Divya was a student of Symbiosis College in Pune who had completed her BBA (Bachelor of Business Administration). Although her family lived in Dubai, she had decided to come to India to study and from there to Canada. So for us, we bonded instantly on our love for Pune city and its student culture.

Amina was the married one who decided to go back to school and complete her post-graduation. She was a hard worker balancing both lives simultaneously. Her husband diligently drops her to college every morning before heading to work himself. She is all praises for him because he has no qualms about her studying further and working, unlike a lot of Bangladeshis back home.

All of us except Divya are focused on our studies, scoring exceedingly well. I tried to do my best to tutor Divya initially, but sensing her disinterest, I stopped.

Our final semester is almost over. On the academic side, I am pretty much sorted as I have already prepared for our mid-term tests. I have a break of about twenty-five days before exams begin. I decide that I would do absolutely nothing but relax and while away my time.

About three days into that plan, I am thoroughly bored out of my wits.

Partly because, unlike me, everyone else is working/studying or busy. It has been a while since I have worked part time as I am occupied with my studies and assignments. To add to my woes, I am also starting to get a little worried about covering my rent for the coming month.

But overall I am great. Hehe.

One late afternoon, I am sitting on the porch of my house having beer, surfing Facebook and contemplating on life in general when I receive a Facebook message from one of my closest friends from engineering days.

Koushik Vutha, a Hyderabadi *potta*, came to Pune like many others to pursue engineering. While I went to VIT (Vishwakarma Institute of Technology), Koushik went to our sister college called VIIT (where the extra 'I' stands for Information). While not being from the same college, we had very similar interests and wasn't long before we hung out with the same groups of friends. We bonded over rock, heavy metal and our dislike for herd mentality. Haha.

Koushik: *Oye bhenchod!* What are you upto *biaatch?* I'm coming to Toronto!

Me: *Charsi saale,* long time! That's awesome timing bro, I'm bored out of my wits.

Koushik: Super! I'm reaching day after, you want anything from London?

Me: Nothing as of now. Awesome! So looking forward to your trip, we will have a blast. For how many days are you coming?

Koushik: Six days, my interim period is on before I dive head on into work! Google, here I come!

Oh, I forgot to mention that Koushik had dropped out of VIIT in the second year. He hated his programme and hence didn't fare too well. Went back to Hyderabad and pursued BCA (Bachelor in Computer application) as he had a knack for programming. He had worked in Wipro for a bit before coming to London to pursue his Master's in Business Intelligence and Analytics.

In his final year, he managed to crack Google. *Ka-ching!*

Me: *Yeaaa! Lezz* do this*!*

On the day of Koushik's arrival, his flight has landed about half an hour in advance. Stepping out through the exit gates, I see Koushik waving. It is awesome to see that *chutiya's* face after a huge gap, and needless to say, we have a lot to catch up on. We hug and I shove a beer in his hand. We decide that we would chill at a pub called The Bull nearby for a bit and kick back a few beers before heading into the city.

We end up staying there about three hours. By the time we leave, it is about 10 p.m. in the night and is still bright as during summers, the days tend to be far longer.

The metro train ride takes us about thirty minutes to get to Danforth station, near my current residence.

We stop by at a supermarket and a LCBO to grab a few sandwiches and beers. Upon entering the house, we see Rod (my Aussie roomie) is up and having a beer himself. We continue the marathon and before we know it, it is almost half past three in the morning. Koushik passes out on the sleeping bag on the floor of my tiny room, while I sit on my laptop, listening to music and planning excursions throughout the city for the coming day. I finally give in and sleep at 4:30 a.m.

At about ten a.m., I am rudely woken up by my phone's vibration.

If there was one sound I hated most in the world, it is the bzzzzz bzzzzzz of a vibrating phone.

It's an unknown number calling.

The guy on the other side introduces himself as Jerry and asks me if I am looking for some part time work. Suddenly, I am wide awake. I could definitely use a bit of cash as month end is nearing and I am cash strapped.

I reply positive to which he replies that he is a party promoter and is organizing a party near the Kipling area of Toronto.

Jerry: "Hi Gavrav, I'm Jerry. I got your reference from my cousin, Vishnu. You worked with him at the Granite Club a while ago. Oh, by the way, how tall are you?"

Me: "Oh, err… Heyaiiie Jerry, it's Gaurav and I'm six feet. Why?"

(Heyaiie is a unique sound made by some people when you want to say hey but end up saying hi. A bit like the high pitched noise made by Bruce Lee when he hits the bad guys.)

Jerry: "Ok, great. You will do, need for protection services at the party."

Me: "Protection services? You mean like a bouncer?"

Jerry: "Yes, come by 6:30 p.m. and I will brief you. The party starts at 8 p.m. I'll text you the address."

Me: "Umm, I haven't ever done something like this before. I don't look too intimidating."

Jerry: "Relax Gavrav, it's an easy street. You only have to frisk folks before they enter."

Me: "Oh. Ok, I'll give it a shot. Is it alright if I get a friend along?"

Jerry: "Sure, as long as he minds his business and doesn't interfere."

Me: "He won't. Don't worry, he's my responsibility."

Jerry: "Sounds good, Gavrav, see you soon."

Although this gig would help cover my house rent a bit, not completely knowing what I am getting myself into, is a strange combination of excitement, curiosity and mortal fear.

I fall asleep after the call. Both of us wake up in the late afternoon and decide to go to a McDonald's nearby for lunch, rent bicycles and go cycling till the place where my gig is. We reach the said location about half hour in advance. The location is closer than I thought.

The address is that of a property which lies behind an enormous gate. I imagine it must be an uber luxurious villa of sorts. We park our bikes outside the gate.

Since there is no one manning the gate, I buzz the video intercom and a man answers from the other end.

Man (rudely): "Yes?"

Me: "Err, Hi! I am here for the bouncer gig? Jerry had called me, today afternoon."

Silence from the other end.

Koushik looks at me and smiles. A smile that says, we should get the fuck out of here. A minute or two later, suddenly, I hear the creaking noise of the gate opening automatically. Standing there, we are stunned whether to go inside or not. Curiosity gets the better of me and I start walking on the cobbled stony pathway leading towards the villa. Koushik follows. The walk from the gate to the villa is very well landscaped and amazingly done. We pass by a small pond filled with swans. Had I not been so pre-occupied with what lies ahead, I would have actually enjoyed the view; absolutely breathtaking.

After what seems like an eternity, actually less than a minute, I arrive at this humongous villa fit for a king.

Or a drug lord.

There are a few mini vans parked outside.

The house has majestic pillars which support the front porch-like area leading to the main door. There are two men talking and upon seeing me, one of them, a curly-haired heavy set guy with South Indian features, smiles and gestures me over.

Man: "Hi, you must be Gavrav? I'm Jerry. Hope this place wasn't too hard to find."

Me: "Hi Jerry, no, not at all. The massive gates are hard to miss. My name's Gau-rav by the way. This is my friend Koushik."

Jerry (extending his hand towards Koushik): "Hey guy! Oh sorry, Gavrav. Also, in case you are wondering how I got your number, Vishnu, my cousin gave it to me. You met him at the Diwali gala at Granite."

Me: "Yup, you mentioned on the phone! I was definitely wondering that. I remember Vishnu, we had an interesting evening, to say the least."

Jerry: "Yes, I heard. He told me that the folks at Granite had fired both you guys despite ya'll doing an excellent job because they were racist. Assholes!"

Aah, Vishnu. You trippy, trippy fucker with a grin!
What tale did you spin?
At the ol' Granite inn?

Me (trying hard not to laugh): "Err, yea, it was bad. Anyway, what do I have to do here? Oh, and is Vishnu coming today?"

Jerry: "No, he's at another gig of mine handling the security detail there. Come, let's go inside."

Vishnu handling security detail! I mean what the actual fuck is the world coming to?!

I follow him inside the ginormous house into what seems like a massive ballroom cum living room type area.

Jerry: "This is where the party will be at. You will stand at the main door there and usher people in after frisking them for any dangerous objects."

Me: "Dangerous objects?"

Jerry: "Yes, weed and a bit of coke is fine, but no guns or knives. Some of the black folks carry that shit literally everywhere. And in case of women, no need to frisk them, only check their purse."

So this was some sort of a high end underground party. For people who were majorly black. Who apparently carried guns and knives. And where I would be the first person in line to get fucked in case something bad happened.

Koushik was giving me the same smile again – the 'we are so fucked' smile. I reciprocated.

Also, I'm not a racist but this initial job description is not helpful at all.

A volley of questions is swirling in my head, coupled with a feeling of throwing up.

Why the fuck don't they hire like a real bouncer?

Someone with real world combat experience who caters to parties where attendees carry weapons.

As if to answer my question, Jerry comes by and hands me an advance for my services.

Jerry: "Licensed bouncers are so bloody expensive now in Toronto. They charge like at least a nine hundred bucks a gig."

Yep, that explains it then.

I was getting paid one hundred and eighty for the whole five to six hours.

One- fifth of the cost at zero skill level.

Hey, it seemed to make sense to him, so who am I to judge! Yup, I'm stupid.

But a stupid person with a few bucks in his pocket is happier than an intelligent person who will be both broke and homeless soon.

And I am determined not to ask for any money from back home in India. After pseudo calculating the risk factor which I have absolutely no idea about, I figure it is alright to do this.

Yup, at the time I am both stupid and logical.

Jerry comes and gives me a black hoodie with skull like logo and 'JJ Events' mentioned on the front and 'Security' on the back.

So, on-door security, it is me and another guy named Farid.

Farid is a beefy guy with the biggest dark circles I've seen in my life. I mean, I first thought that he had just woken up and showed up here.

Also, he doesn't talk much and merely grumbles when spoken to, except for when he tells me that I need to stand in front and frisk people while he will 'watch over me'.

Well, being Farid, his words are a bit more monosyllabic in nature.

"You pat 'em, I'm here."

That's it. That's all he has said.

So, yes, as you've guessed by now, I am pretty much on my own. Koushik goes inside the house to explore.

Around fifteen past eight, the music starts inside the house and I can feel the buzz of the bass outside. The music is primarily hip hop, RnB and Drum&Bass.

The deejay starts off playing mellow tunes which helps take the edge off my current predicament. Grooving to the music, time passes by swiftly and soon, I see the cars start trickling in around 9 p.m.

I take my position while Farid takes his 'behind me', holding the entry stamp.

Jerry drops by and whispers in my ear to not let anyone inside till he says so. Conveying the message, I ask the guests to line up. Soon, I see him giving me a thumbs up to start allowing guests to enter. The first guest which I frisk is this super built hulk of a guy who seems Jamaican with massive dreadlocks. Patting him down, my hands are trembling with fear but he seems unperturbed. He smiles looking at me and enters without a word. A tiny girl accompanies him carrying a giant purse. I check her purse and she enters too. All's well so far.

Soon, I am through with checking almost all the lined up guests without any incident. Except a few women sniggering and asking me as to why I am not patting them down also.

Surprisingly, the only dangerous item I find is a small knife in a woman's purse. No guns. Phew!

The party starts at a full swing and the house is pretty packed by half past ten. Jerry swings by a while later and hands me a pint of beer. Koushik is with him.

He does not give one to Farid but instead instructs him to take my position.

He tells Farid that a few VIP guests would be coming by soon and that he is to simply let them in without frisking them. He nudges me to follow him inside the venue. I hand my beer to Farid who looks like his dark circles are increasing in size by the minute. He could really use a beer or two.

Jerry whispers in my ear that I can relax now and let Farid be on duty outside as most people have arrived. I am absolutely thrilled.

Koushik: "Bro, I am feeling super hungry. Let's find something to eat here."

Me: "Let's do it!"

We haven't eaten anything post lunch and head inside the house to find something to eat. I have tunnel vision now and am only searching for food because all I can see everywhere is just drinks. Just before the main ballroom/living room area, I see a smaller room whose door is ajar. Koushik has already walked ahead into the ballroom.

The room is mostly filled with plants and there is a table lined with a few peanut butter sandwiches. I am extremely famished so I wolf down a sandwich. Although they taste a bit stale, having a slightly bitter after-taste, my hunger ignores the same. Koushik soon joins in and we finish at least two to three sandwiches each.

Satisfied, we sit on the ground inside the room, talking about old memories. I get this urge to enter the main living room area to check out the party. Koushik too wants to get out of the dingy room and we make our way towards the main ballroom. Upon entering, the vibe is simply electric. The deejay is playing exceptional music and everyone is completely zoned in to the tunes he's belting out.

I am ecstatic. I start dancing and grooving as the music is hypnotizing to say the least.

My stomach starts to slightly cramp up and gives a tingling sensation.

I am thinking, I should not have eaten stale food as my stomach gets upset easily.

But the music and the dancing seem to be healing in a way, so I continue to dance to the tunes, giving in completely to the flow of music. I have attended a few gigs by famous DJs, belting out amazing tunes, but this night is something else. This one, although, I forgot his name, like a magician, astonishes everyone, one track after another.

113

The ceiling of the room has a huge disco ball reflecting lights across the room. I am admiring the sheer size of the thing when suddenly, it seems like that ball is increasing in size.

It keeps getting bigger and I can see each shiny glass square on it in detail along with the colours that glass square is reflecting.

I haven't seen something which looks so beautiful in my life. It's like someone has turned on HD television mode for my vision. All around me, I see happy faces with smiles, each colour, extremely vivid and detailed and an absolute treat to see.

Although my mind is thoroughly confused as to what is happening. Extremely happy, but confused.

Seeing Koushik's face in the crowd relaxes me a bit and I decide to go to him. He seems to be blabbering something and pointing towards the ceiling.

I finally make sense as to what he's saying. He is admiring the giant disco ball on the ceiling, pointing the various details. I look up and I see what he means.

We are standing there in the middle of the dance floor, discussing the various aspects and the beauty of a disco ball.

Before we know it, we have been paid, have left the party and are walking towards our bikes. Just before reaching the gate, we stop to admire the swans that are sleeping with their heads tucked into their feathers on their back, floating on water. The view is something else.

Koushik: "I haven't seen such beauty in my life. But, those sandwiches, yuck!! If I wasn't that hungry, I wouldn't have eaten them."

Me: "Bro, I think I know what's happening to us. I think we are tripping. And I am pretty sure it was those sandwiches!"

Koushik: "Tripping? You mean Mushrooms! Ohhh fuck, it makes sense!"

Me: "Haan bhai, no wonder we are seeing everything in such detail. It is absolutely breathtaking. I've read that a mushroom trip usually lasts about five to six hours. Let's get our bikes and roll."

Koushik: "Woooow, let's ride on!"

We get on our bikes and start riding. It feels a little woozy and off balance as I am riding, but slowly I get the hang of it.

Koushik seems to be struggling, stopping and putting his feet down every ten seconds.

The beauty of the world is something else tonight. It is still bright with about another hour of daylight left and everything I look at is mesmerizing.

Kipling has a lake nearby so we ride towards the lakeshore. At least a dozen seagulls are just flying around, literally, in slow motion.

Every time a seagull flies over us, I could zoom in to see in great detail what it looks like, up high.

It is like we have a super power to zoom into things, see everything around us in great detail, including colours and textures.

There is a rather large boat dock on the lake and we just stop to admire at it. What a beauty!

With its deep red hull, shining white interior, it is a masterpiece.

Me: "Dude, this is the most amazing thing I have ever seen. I mean, look at the light bouncing off the bow! It is magnificient!!"

Koushik: "So, I'm wearing a hat right. The girl is wearing this white long dress, her arms around me, I am sailing bro, sailing into paradise!"

Me (thinking *kya chutiya baatein kar raha hai* Koushik): "What?! No, bro, not the girl, see the boat. See it properly, you will be mind blown!"

Koushik: "Ya,I get it, but see, she is standing next to me, her hair flowing in the wind. I'm the captain, she's my lady. I'm seeing this entire dude, this is amazing! I am now steering the boat, making a turn here..."

Me (tuning out what Koushik is saying and blabbering on my own): "....The cabin looks nice, those sofas inside, wow!

Wish I was a millionaire, I would definitely buy this right here, right now!"

And this goes on for another half an hour.

As you've guessed by now, we are tripping balls.

A while later, we start riding our bikes again. As I am riding next to the road, I see a car stopping at the signal right across us.

I zoom in to see the guy inside the car. He's playing a really trippy rap song and I can see him with one arm outstretched holding the steering. His hand has a blingy watch and his face with his big sunglasses has a placid expression as he waits for the light to turn green. Ultimate swag!

The entire scene with the music, the guy and his expression makes me imagine myself inside a Fifty Cent video. It is like I am watching television but I am inside the TV.

If that makes sense.

Yup, it sure doesn't.

This is 'experience-every-thing-live' TV!

My bike has transformed into a chromed version of itself with shiny gold rims and cool retro handlebars. Excited by this visual, I want to show Koushik what I just saw and want him to experience the same. I swivel my head around to call Koushik. But for the umpteenth time, Koushik has almost fallen off his bike again.

This time, another biker almost hits him. I realize that it's very unsafe for us to keep riding our bikes as our trip has come on pretty strong and we might hurt ourselves. So, we decide to walk with our bikes tagging alongside till we find a spot where we can lock both of them. Now, we walk.

Without a plan, or a destination in sight.

As the mighty shrooms are our guide tonight.

About half a kilometre later, we find a pole and padlock our bikes to it. I am feeling much better and lighter as the weight of lugging/pushing the bikes around has lifted. I click a photo of the street name and the intersection where we have parked our bikes, just in case we forget.

I feel happy and giddy in my stomach as the mushroom digests further and releases its magic juices. We are now in our third hour. We continue our journey into the unknown, stopping frequently whenever we see something beautiful, unique or bizarre. Both I and Koushik are pretty much in sync when we stop to see something. It is like, our trip is somehow connected and we are tripping over the exact same things.

Albeit with our own rendition of the same.

It all sounds too philosophical now in my head. But at that time, it makes sense for some reason.

Meandering along, we stumble upon a small group of classical musicians playing outside a pub.

Our guide has brought us here to enjoy this unique musical extravaganza. Each musician is deeply engrossed in what they are playing. The band has four members with one guy playing the cello while the others playing the violin. Their music fills me up with happiness and makes me thank god for music. In life in general, I have always been fascinated and an admirer of all kinds of music. Be it heavy metal, rock, house, psy, dubstep, classical, country, even Bollywood. My friends are almost always on one side of the fence, discussing the other genres.

Tonight, I think that deep rooted interest of mine has been magnified.

It is truly bliss listening to them play.

I am especially fascinated by the guy playing the big cello. The deep bass notes are really standing out and with each variation in sound, the size of the cello keeps dilating in front of me.

I zoom in to focus on the guy's fingers as they move flawlessly over the instrument. They continue playing their set while Koushik and I are taking it all in, loving the journey they have set us upon. There are a few people who are wearing t-shirts with aliens printed on them, similar to the ones I've seen in Goa, India.

Although now, the aliens are alive, dancing or bobbing their little heads to the music. I never knew the significance of this ever when I was in Goa as I had never done psychedelics, only loads of alcohol. I used to see a lot of people there, tripping on cool looking paintings of aliens, complex art forms and I could never understand as to why it was so enjoyable for them.

Now, however, I have a slight glimpse of the grass on the other side.

And it sure is greener.

Out of the corner of my eye, there is something making me very uneasy. There is someone who is constantly staring at us and telling his friends something due to which his friends are laughing.

They are pointing fingers at us, giggling.

My trip takes a complete U- turn from being super positive and great, to depressing. I start to get paranoid and want to get the hell out of there.

Daylight is now almost gone and the skies are a shade of dark purple.

Suddenly, we can feel rain start to pour and thunder roar through the skies.

A lot changed in the last few minutes!

I can see that Koushik is as flabbergasted as I am, to the whims of nature.

Both of us are depressed as fuck, as shrooms were playing their full part in amplifying our core emotions which at the time is sadness.

We run for cover inside a book store nearby.

Koushik: "What the fuck just happened, it was nice and sunny just a few minutes ago!"

Me: "I'm so sorry man, *chutiya ban gaye hum*. Wish we hadn't eaten those stupid mushrooms. I feel like crap!"

Koushik: "I know, and we are a long way from home, I want to go home man, what am I doing here!"

Me (trying to snap out of it, but in vain): "Let's get a cab; we are too tripped out to go by the metro. We will collect our bikes tomorrow morning."

Koushik: "Whatever bhai, I want to go home! This country is worse than London."

From inside the store, I hail a cab which stops right outside. We quickly bolt inside and ask the driver to go to Danforth.

I feel infinitely better now that I'm inside the taxi, on my way home.

And the driver has a calm energy to him which helps us get off our bad trip.

Me: "Finally, we are on our way, don't worry, it will be over soon. What a day this has been!"

Koushik: "I know! Feel so much better now bro, but still quite depressed."

Driver: "*Aap log India se ho?*"

Me (surprised at the sudden question in Hindi): "*Haan bhaiya, main Mumbai se hoon, aur yeh Hyderabad. Aap kahan se ho?*"

Driver: "Pakistan."

Me: "Oh. *Kitne saal se ho aap yahan?*"

Driver: "*Meri toh ab poori zindagi ho gayi hai yahan pe. Main ek martaba* Mumbai *aaya tha, badiya sheher hai, log bahut* helpful *hai. Aapke naam kya hai? Main bata nahi sakta hoon, ke aap ke saath apni bhaasha mein baat karke kitna acha lag raha hai.*"

Me: "Haha, *haan woh toh hai bhaiya, apni bhaasha ka apna hi mazaa hai. Main* Gaurav *hoon aur yeh* Koushik. *Aap kahan aaye the* Mumbai *mein?*"

Driver: "*Main* Borivali *mein aaya tha, mere kuch dost rehte the wahan. Unnis so nabbe* (1990) *mein, shayad aap bahut chote honge tabhi.*"

Me: "*Ji bhaiya.*"

Driver: "*Mujhe toh* Indians *se bahut pyaar hai. Kitne khushmisaaj log hote hain. Hamesha pyaar se baat karte hain. Humaare yahan bhi, itni hi shiddat se baat karte hain. Hum bahut ache log hain* Gaurav *ji, joh mehemaano ko saraakhon pe rakhte hain. Kabhi aap ek dafah* Pakistan *jaayiye, aapko itna pyaar milega, ke aap khud hairaan hojayenge. Lekin duniya humse darrti hai kyunki kuch log hai humare desh mein, joh tabaahi aur deheshat ke ilaawa kuch nahi karte. Hum khud unnse pareshaan hain, lekin hum bhi kya karen?*"

Me: "Wow *bhaiya, aap bhi yeh sochte hain? Aap pehele insaan hai* Pakistan *se jisse main iss baare mein baat kar raha hoon.*"

Driver: "*Jo sach hai, who sach hai. Aapki tarah, hum bhi unnko utna hi naapasand karte hain, gaali bhi dete hain, lekin duniya ke saamne, hum ek hi hain.*"

Me: "*Aap ki baatein sun kar main hairaan hoon.* We had our own opinions according to what the news channels showed us and we are programmed to believe growing up."

Driver: "Yes, hence I am telling you this. There is always another side to every story. We want to show our love to people but are afraid as people have already judged us based on the bias created by the few. But every chance we get, we do not fail to show our affection and *khaatirdaari*.But I'll tell you another thing. Back home, people think that I am living a great life in this beautiful country, earning good money. But sir, let me tell you, *main yahan hoon yeh meri majboori hai, zarurat nahi*. I am like a bird trapped in a golden cage, whose world although is beautiful inside the cage, is ultimately trapped in it's own existence.

"Whatever people say about the western countries, there is one thing no one talks about here. It's the loneliness. It is an epidemic which no one speaks about, especially men, as modern society looks at it as a sign of weakness. In life, always remember, chase your hopes and dreams, but make sure you also chase a well-rounded life with plenty of friends and loved ones, who will give it meaning beyond material desires."

Koushik, who although is silent throughout our ride home, is hanging on to every word he was saying.

So am I.

For us, it is a conversation with a godly being.

An infinitely wise old man who calls a spade, a spade.

Soon, the car pulls over outside our house. Although the journey time is about forty minutes, it feels like we have travelled for hours and hours.

Driver: "*Aap dono se mil ke bahut achha laga. Khuda aap ko apne hifz-o-amaan mein rakhe.*"

Koushik (shaking the driver's hand): "*Aap se bhi mil ke bahut achchha laga, bhaiya. Aap ne apna naam nahi bataya?*"

Driver: "..."

To this day, neither me nor Koushik can recall his name.

Epilogue

$\mathcal{G}$reetings, kind reader.

Hope you have enjoyed reading this book.

This is something which I have been meaning to write since a while but being a hobby writer, it takes time to put thoughts on paper or MS Word.

Writing is incredibly liberating, especially experiential writing in my case, as it allows you to dig deep within your psyche, pull out that memory/story which created that unforgettable experience for you and pen it down.

Simply through words, you are inviting someone to be a part of your journey and experience the highs and lows with you.

Being an introvert by nature, I would have difficulty in group situations, striking conversations with people I don't know, public speaking or even general confidence in myself. A thing which I discovered about myself through my collective experiences is that I have a burning desire to eliminate each and every fear of mine from the root.

Living in Canada on my own made me the person I am today.

It has taught me perseverance, value of money, humility and an inherent fearlessness, i.e. being able to pursue whatever I like without the fear of the unknown, without preconceived notions and also without the fear of what others might think.

This is what I believe has contributed to my success today as an entrepreneur. All these factors combined are what are required for success in any field.

I had a well-paying job in Toronto which I quit to return to Indian to pursue my dream of starting my own business. My parents were supportive of that decision, for which I cannot thank them enough.

I started 'LittleFlorist.com' with an investment of thirty thousand rupees from my own savings. It is an online florist which allows customers to send flowers and gifts across India to their loved ones.

Since flowers are a perishable commodity, one cannot courier the flower bouquets. They have to be sourced locally.

Each day, I would wake up and make cold calls to flower vendors across India, asking them to join my platform. Most of them are apprehensive initially to join a newbie like me with no experience.

But I kept at it.

I knew that sooner than later, there will be someone who will come on board. And soon enough, they did.

On my eighth day of trying, I managed to onboard twenty vendors from six cities in a single day!

With each vendor that I added, it became successively easier to add the next one as I could tell him about the people I already had on board. Within the span of a month, I had over one hundred and seventy vendors across seventy cities in India.

Flowers, cakes and gifts could now be delivered by Little Florist to all those cities. I also added same day and midnight delivery as a service.

In the little spare time that I got, I learnt Photoshop and Google Adwords as I could not afford to hire anyone to do the creatives or marketing for me.

Soon, D day arrived and Little Florist was a go.

I played multiple roles during those initial days, right from an operations manager, a graphic designer, a marketing executive and a delivery boy.

In my first month, I made a profit of twenty-five thousand rupees. I was ecstatic to say the least.

In my third month since inception, on Valentine's Day I did a profit of sixty-five thousand rupees in a single day.

I was profitable within the first few months itself as I had very little overheads. I also got an opportunity to supply fresh flowers to a premier five star hotel, which added to my monthly revenue.

After a year, I saw that for some reason, flower bouquet sales had hit a plateau. Even though I was doing a good number of orders each month, the growth had slowed considerably.

Being bootstrapped, I did not have very high marketing budgets.

Year two of Little Florist was difficult as I could see a massive shift in people's perceptions of gifting flowers in general, thereby affecting my core business model. I saw that since I did not have a big USP for my brand, my business would sink if I did not do anything soon.

After much deliberation, I decided to explore new verticals in the field.

Diversification is the key, I thought. That year was spent exploring different options for my brand, most of which failed miserably. For each failure, I got my fair share of advice and concerns from loved ones.

Their concern was usually along the lines of 'what I would do in the future' as this was going nowhere.

Their concerns manifested into my thoughts, as I too started second guessing myself if I should start applying for jobs if Little Florist did not make it. I had to let go of some of my most competent staff as I could not afford to pay them.

But, I realized something. Despite all failures, there wasn't a single moment when I felt that I should quit or was simply tired of doing what I was doing.

I loved doing business!

This was my calling, plain and simple. And that there weren't a lot of people my age, including my friends, who were doing the kind of things I was doing and taking the kind of risks I was taking.

A few notable pursuits for Little Florist that year included a franchise model where Little Florist would open franchises for interested investors looking to start a new business.

I opened a franchise in Lucknow and Solapur.

Another was a tie up with India's biggest gifting brand 'Archies'.

Although both of them were well received initially, they too hit a brick wall.

Only one vertical which was doing fairly decent was the B2B one, i.e. supply of fresh flowers to hotels.

It was something which I had overlooked as I was simply focusing on my core B2C model.

Change is essential if one must survive and succeed. I shifted my entire focus to that vertical.

I went from the customer to the source and started building relationships with the growers, importers and suppliers of fresh flowers.

My vendor on-boarding experience helped immensely and soon, JP Agro, my flower supply firm, is now one of the biggest suppliers of flowers to premier five star hotels in Mumbai, Pune and Delhi.

After JP Agro, I wanted to pursue something in the media and digital advertising space. During whatever free time that I had, I started devoting to understanding the depths of social media, how it influences, how it is measured, basically the analytical side of it. I even did a short stint as a Media Sales Executive at a company to fully understand how it works. Digital media became something which I grew really fond of and wanted to start something in this space.

Enter Hansika Chandiramani, aka my wife.

She had been a celebrity manager for quite a few renowned celebrities and during our dating phase we realized that both of us were quite passionate and motivated in our respective fields. We decided to setup a company together called HC Media named after her.

And we started HC Media in our dating phase!

Working with a partner who is also your wife comes with its own share of responsibilities, failures, successes, knacks, ups and downs. With me handling the digital brand advocacy side of the company and Hansika handling the live events and endorsement side of it, slowly but surely we are expanding into different aspects of a full service celebrity management agency with a range of exclusive artists.

Both Hansika and I are people who love to have fun while working hard and enjoying what we do.

Even when we got married, we decided to do something which was never done before in India.

Hansika came up with this brilliant idea of getting brands on board for our wedding, giving way to India's first 'Branded Wedding'. Everything from alcohol to makeup to clothing, etc., was sponsored by brands.

You can check out our viral branded wedding video on YouTube.

It's called Band Baajaa and Brands! (The Unconventional Wedding) and our channel name is Super Desi.

So, I end with this note:

Passionate individuals are never bogged down by failure itself as they love what they do.

But their spirit is definitely shattered by people's perception of his/her failure and the negative connotation attached to that word.

People, due to their deep fear for failure, try to dissuade others from failing.

Their fear of what could happen makes nothing happen for them.

They never experience anything new.

They never learn.

They never grow.

I feel that failure is the most positive thing that can happen to a person. It is the most effective teacher whose lessons are embedded within you for a lifetime. It helps you understand yourself more, discover aspects of your psyche which only help you succeed and take situations head on.

No amount of education in the world can teach you that.

Once you get this out of the way, your brain becomes clearer to focus, enjoy and digest the scenario at hand.

And that is what life is truly all about.

Discovering yourself through experiences, making memories and doing what you love.

Because when you do what you love, you will never work a day in your life :)